Soon the prince found himself in John Canty's house, with the door closed. By the dim light of a candle in a bottle, he saw his dismal surroundings, and also its occupants.

Two messy girls and a middle-aged woman cowered in one corner, like tortured animals who expected more abuse. From another corner came a withered hag with gray hair and evil eyes. John Canty said to her: "Wait! There is treasure here. Do nothing until you've heard. Then let your hand be as heavy as you like. Come here, lad. Now say your ridiculous things again, if you haven't forgotten. Say your name. Who are you?"

The prince blushed again at the insult. He lifted a steady and indignant gaze to the man's face, and said: "You show your bad upbringing by commanding me to speak. I tell you now, as I told you before, I am Edward, Prince of Wales."

A Note about
The Prince and the Pauper

The Prince and the Pauper begins in 1537, at the births of Edward VI, an actual historical figure, and Tom Canty, a fictional character. The main action then leaps to 1547, when both boys are 10 years old. King Henry VIII is on the throne of England, but he is about to die. His son, Edward VI, should take his place. However, just a few hours before Henry's death, Edward meets and switches places with the pauper Tom.

This period of England's history is known as the Tudor period. It was an era full of extremes: cruel laws, outrageous wealth, crippling poverty. There was an expansive gap between the rich and poor classes, and almost no one went back and forth between these two worlds. This is part of what makes Tom and Edward's tale so unusual.

The reader should keep in mind that the novel is set in a real time and place, and, therefore, it is limited by certain historical facts. For example, the author, Mark Twain, cannot change the date of the king's coronation. However, Twain is able to imagine, within the historical limits, what *might* have happened to his characters.

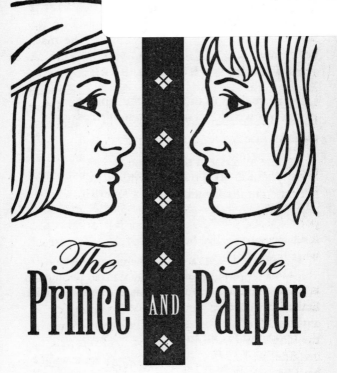

The
Prince AND Pauper

Edited, with an Afterword,
by Mary Ann Fugate

TP THE TOWNSEND LIBRARY

THE PRINCE AND THE PAUPER

TP **THE TOWNSEND LIBRARY**

For more titles in the Townsend Library,
visit our website: **www.townsendpress.com**

All new material in this edition is
copyright © 2004 by Townsend Press.
Printed in the United States of America

0 9 8 7 6 5 4 3 2

Illustrations © 2004 by Hal Taylor

Townsend Press, Inc.
439 Kelley Drive
West Berlin, New Jersey 08091

ISBN-13: 978-1-59194-015-9
ISBN-10: 1-59194-015-X

Library of Congress Control Number:
2003105798

TABLE OF CONTENTS

CHAPTER 1

The Birth of
the Prince and the Pauper

In old London on an autumn day in the six-teenth century, a boy was born to the poor Canty family, who did not want him. On the same day, another English child was born to the rich Tudor family, who did want him; in fact, all of England was overjoyed about his birth. There was much celebration throughout the nation. Everyone, rich or poor, spent several days feasting, dancing, and singing. London came alive with colorful banners, splendid parades, and evening bonfires. The only thing people talked about was the baby Edward Tudor, Prince of Wales, who lay wrapped in silk, unaware of his importance. Tom Canty, however, wore only rags, and he did not give anyone, even his family, cause for celebration.

CHAPTER 2

Tom's Early Life

Tom Canty spent his childhood in a ramshackle neighborhood near London Bridge. The streets were narrow, crooked, and dirty. The neighborhood's houses were built so that their upper stories hung out over the street below. Their wooden beams were painted in different colors, which gave them a certain charm. Shaped like small diamonds, their windows opened out on hinges, like doors.

Tom's family lived in one room of a cramped, crumbling house on Offal Court, off Pudding Lane. Tom's parents slept in a bed in the corner. Tom, his grandmother, and his two sisters, Bet and Nan, slept on the floor. Every night, they made their beds from a pile of blankets and dirty straw. In the morning they threw the bedding back in a heap.

Bet and Nan were fifteen-year-old twins. They were goodhearted girls but unclean, dressed in rags, and extremely ignorant, like their mother. Their father and grandmother were wicked and cruel. They cursed constantly and got drunk whenever they could; then they fought each other or anyone else who came their way. John Canty was a thief, and his mother a beggar. They forced the children to beg, too.

Another person who lived in the house was an old priest named Father Andrew, whom the king had forced to retire with a small pension. Father Andrew secretly taught the children right from wrong. He also taught Tom a little Latin, and how to read and write. He would have done the same with the girls, but they were afraid that their friends would make fun of them for becoming educated.

The other houses on the street were as crowded as Tom's. People drank, fought, and rioted all night, and they often injured one another.

Little Tom was not unhappy. His life was hard, but he did not know it. It was the sort of life that all the Offal Court boys had, so he thought it was normal. When he came home empty-handed at night, he knew that his father would curse and beat him and that his awful grandmother would do the same, more viciously. Later his starving mother would sneak him a tiny bit of food that she had saved by going hungry herself, even though she usually was caught in the act and beaten for it by her husband.

Tom's life went along well enough, especially in summer. He begged only enough to scrape by, because he didn't want to increase his chances of being arrested and punished. He spent most of his time listening to good Father Andrew's charming old tales and legends about giants and fairies, dwarves and genies, enchanted castles, and gorgeous kings and princes. His head became full of these wonderful things. At night, as he lay in the dark on his dirty straw, feeling tired, hungry, and sore from a beating, he forgot his aches and pains by imagining the charmed life of a spoiled prince in a regal palace. He found himself longing to see a real prince. He spoke of it once to some of his friends, but they teased him so mercilessly that he never mentioned it to them again.

He often read the priest's old books and asked him to talk about them. These readings and discussions made Tom wish for a different life, and eventually his behavior started to change. He began to act like the prince he dreamed of meeting. His speech and gestures became more formal, and he cared more for his appearance. Although he still enjoyed playing in the mud, he used water from the Thames River to wash himself afterwards.

At first Tom's friends laughed at these changes, but gradually they began to admire him for being so educated and capable. They thought that he was full of knowledge and wisdom. The children reported Tom's talents to their parents, who also began to see the boy as something special. Soon adults brought their problems to Tom, and they often were astonished at the wit and wisdom of his decisions. He quickly became a hero to all who knew him except his own family, who saw him as ordinary.

After a while Tom privately organized a royal court. He was the prince; his best friends were guards, lords and ladies in waiting, and the royal family. Every day, the court performed complicated ceremonies that Tom borrowed from the books he had read. The royal council also met to discuss the kingdom's business, and Tom gave orders to his imaginary armies and navies. Afterward the pretend prince would leave, wearing his same old clothes, and beg a little money. After eating some scraps of food and enduring another beating, he would stretch out on his pile of dirty straw and return to his imaginary world. Tom's desire to see a real prince became stronger with every passing day. Eventually he forgot everything but this goal, and it became his life's one passion.

One rainy January day, during his usual begging tour, he walked sadly up and down the area near Mincing Lane and Little East Cheap. Barefoot and cold, he spent hours looking through bakery windows, longing for the vile pork pies and other unhealthy food displayed there. To him, these smelled like heavenly morsels that he never had been lucky enough to eat. At night Tom reached home so wet, tired, and hungry that even his father and grandmother felt sorry for him. So they hit him only a few times and sent him to bed.

For a while his pain and hunger, and the swearing and fighting going on in the building, kept him awake. At last his thoughts drifted to faraway, romantic lands, and he fell asleep dreaming of jeweled princes in giant palaces, with servants who rushed to carry out their orders. As usual, he dreamed that he was a prince himself. All night long he enjoyed the luxury of royal life. He walked with great lords and ladies, smelling perfumes and listening to delightful music while acknowledging the respectful greetings of the crowd as it parted to make way for him.

When he awoke from his dream in the morning and saw the misery around him, his real life seemed worse than ever. Then came bitterness, heartbreak, and tears.

CHAPTER 3

Tom's Meeting with the Prince

Tom got up hungry, and he left the house hungry, but his thoughts were busy with all the wonderful dreams from the night before. He wandered here and there in the city, hardly noticing where he was going or what was happening around him. People jostled him and some said mean things, but he was too distracted to pay attention.

Eventually he found himself at Temple Bar, the farthest from home he ever had traveled in that direction. He stopped and considered a moment, then fell into his daydreams again and passed beyond London's walls. The Strand changed from a country road to a street, but just barely. Although there was a compact row of houses on one side, there were only a few mansions on the street's other side. These impressive buildings stood on acres that stretched all the way down to the river. Today this land is packed with small houses.

Soon Tom discovered Charing Village, and he stopped at the beautiful cross built there by a grieving king of earlier days. Then he strolled down a quiet, lovely road, past the great cardinal's dignified palace, toward a far mightier and more majestic palace: Westminster. Tom stared in wonder at its vast stonework, wide wings, intimidating towers, and huge stone gateways, with their golden bars and enormous granite lions and other symbols of English royalty. Was his soul's desire to be satisfied at last? Here, indeed, was a king's palace. Could he hope to see a prince now, a flesh-and-blood prince?

At each side of the golden gate stood a guard, clad in shining armor, who resembled a statue. At a respectful distance were many country folk and city people, waiting for a glimpse of royalty. Splendid carriages, with splendid people in them and splendid servants outside, were arriving and departing by several other gateways to the royal courtyard.

Poor little Tom approached in his rags and was moving slowly and timidly past the guards, with a beating heart and rising hope, when he saw something through the golden bars that almost made him shout for joy. Inside was a handsome boy, tan from outdoor exercise, whose silk and satin clothing shone with jewels. He wore a little jeweled sword and dagger at his hip, elegant red-heeled boots, and a dashing crimson cap with drooping feathers fastened with a great sparkling gem. Several gorgeous gentlemen stood nearby— his servants, no doubt. Oh! He was a true, living prince. The prayer of the pauper boy's heart was answered. Tom's breath came quick and short with excitement, and his eyes grew big with wonder and delight. His mind focused on one desire: to get close to the prince and have a good look at him.

Before he knew what he was doing, he had his face against the gate's bars. The next instant, one of the soldiers snatched him away and sent him spinning among the staring crowd of country simpletons and London idlers. The soldier said, "Mind your manners, you young beggar!" The crowd jeered and laughed, but the young prince, his face flushed and his eyes flashing with anger, sprang to the gate and cried out, "How dare you use a poor lad like that! How dare you use the king, my father's meanest subject in such a way! Open the gates and let him in." You should have seen that unpredictable crowd snatch off their hats then. You should have heard them cheer and shout, "Long live the Prince of Wales!"

The soldiers saluted with their long axes, opened the gates, and saluted again as the little Prince of Poverty passed in, wearing his fluttering rags, to join hands with the Prince of Limitless Plenty. Edward Tudor said, "You look tired and hungry; you have been treated badly. Come with me." Half a dozen attendants sprang forward to interfere, but they were waved aside with a royal gesture, and they stopped, frozen where they were like so many statues.

Edward took Tom to a rich apartment in the palace. At his command a meal was brought in such as Tom never had known except in books. The prince, with princely grace and manners, sent the servants away so that their critical presence would not embarrass his humble guest. Then he sat nearby and asked questions while Tom ate.

"What is your name, lad?"

"Tom Canty, if it please you, sir."

"That's an odd name. Where do you live?"

"In the city, sir. Offal Court, out of Pudding Lane."

"Offal Court. That's another odd name. Do you have parents?"

"I have parents, sir, and a grandmother, but she is not dear to me (God forgive me if it is wrong to say that). Also twin sisters, Nan and Bet."

"Your grandmother is not too kind to you, I take it."

"Or to anyone else, your worship. She has a wicked heart and does evil all her days."

"Does she mistreat you?"

"There are times, when she is asleep or overcome with drink, that she doesn't mistreat me. But when she is sober again, she makes it up to me with hearty beatings."

A fierce look came into the little prince's eyes, and he cried out, "What? Beatings?"

"Yes, sir."

"Beatings! And you so frail and little. Listen: before night comes, she will go to the Tower. The king, my father..."

"You forget her low ranking, sir. The Tower is

for nobles only."

"True. I had not thought of that. I will consider her punishment. Is your father kind to you?"

"Not more than Grandmother Canty, sir."

"Fathers are alike perhaps. Mine does not have a sweet temper. He hits with a heavy hand but spares me. He does not always spare me with his tongue, though. How does your mother treat you?"

"She is good, sir, and gives me no sorrow or pain. Nan and Bet are similar."

"How old are they?"

"Fifteen, sir."

"Lady Elizabeth, my sister, is fourteen, and Lady Jane Grey, my cousin, is my age and beautiful and gracious. But my sister Lady Mary, with her gloomy face and—look, do your sisters forbid their servants to smile, so that the sin does not destroy their souls?"

"My sisters? Do you think, sir, that they have servants?"

The little prince contemplated the little pauper a moment, then asked, "Why not? Who helps them undress at night? Who dresses them when they rise?"

"No one, sir. Should they sleep without their garment, like the beasts?"

"Their garment? Have they only one?"

"Yes, your worship. What would they do with more? They have only one body each."

"A quaint and marvelous thought. Pardon, I

didn't mean to laugh. Your good Nan and Bet soon will have plenty of clothes and servants. My accountant will see to it. No, do not thank me. It's nothing. You speak well and gracefully. Are you educated?"

"I do not know if I am or not, sir. A good priest called Father Andrew taught me, out of kindness, from his books."

"Do you know Latin?"

"Only a little, sir."

"Learn it, lad. It's hard only at first. Greek is harder. But neither these nor any other languages, I think, are hard for Lady Elizabeth and my cousin. You should hear those damsels speak. But tell me of Offal Court. Do you have a pleasant life there?"

"Yes, sir, except when I'm hungry. There are Punch-and-Judy shows and monkeys—such playful creatures and so well-dressed! There are plays in which the actors shout and fight until all are killed, and it's fine to see. It costs only a farthing, although it's very hard to get the farthing, please your worship."

"Tell me more."

"We lads of Offal Court duel each other with fighting sticks, as though we were soldiers."

The prince's eyes flashed. He said, "Indeed, I would like that. Tell me more."

"We compete in races, sir, to see which of us is fastest."

"I would like that also. Speak on."

"In summer, sir, we wade and swim in the canals and river, and duck and splash each other with water, and dive and shout and tumble and..."

"It would be worth my father's kingdom to enjoy it only once. Please go on."

"We dance and sing around the Maypole in Cheapside. We play in the sand; we cover each other with sand. Sometimes we make mud pastry. Oh, the lovely mud! It is more fun than anything else in the world."

"Please say no more. It's glorious. If only I could dress in clothes like yours, and bare my feet, and play in the mud once, just once, with no one to scold or forbid me, I believe I could give up the crown!"

"And if I could dress, sweet sir, as you are dressed, just once..."

"Oh, would you like it? Then so be it. Take off your rags, and put on these splendors, lad. It is a brief happiness, but it will be intense. We will have it while we may and change again before anyone bothers us."

A few minutes later the little Prince of Wales was decorated with Tom's fluttering odds and ends, and the little Prince of Pauperdom was tricked out in the gaudy outfit of royalty. The two stood side by side before a great mirror and saw a miracle: no change seemed to have been made! They stared at each other, then at the glass, then at each other again. At last the puzzled prince asked, "What do you make of this?"

"Your worship, please don't require me to answer. It is not proper that a person of my rank should say."

"Then I will answer. You have the same hair, same eyes, same voice and manner, same build, same face and expression. If we went naked, no one could say which was you and which the Prince of Wales. Now that I am clothed as you were clothed, I would be able to feel the way you did when the brute soldier... Is that a bruise on your hand?"

"Yes, but it is small, and your worship knows that the poor guard..."

"Enough! It was a shameful and cruel thing!"

the little prince cried, stamping his bare foot. "If the king... Do not move until I come back. It is a command."

Within a moment he snatched up and put away an article of national importance that lay on a table, hurried out the door, and was flying across the palace grounds in his fluttering rags, with a hot face and glowing eyes. As soon as he reached the great gate, he grabbed the bars and tried to shake them, shouting, "Open! Unbar the gates!"

The soldier who had mistreated Tom promptly obeyed. As the prince burst through the opening, half smothered with royal wrath, the soldier gave him a blow on the ear that sent him whirling to the roadway and said, "Take that, beggar's spawn, for what you got me from his highness."

The crowd roared with laughter. The prince picked himself out of the mud and charged at the sentry, shouting, "I am the Prince of Wales. My body is sacred, and you will hang for laying your hand on me!"

The soldier brought his long ax to a salute and said mockingly, "I salute your gracious highness." Then he added angrily, "Be off, you crazy rubbish!"

The jeering crowd closed around the poor little prince and hustled him far down the road, hooting at him and shouting, "Make way for his royal highness! Make way for the Prince of Wales!"

CHAPTER 4

The Prince's Troubles Begin

After hours of persecution the crowd left the little prince to himself. As long as he had raged against the mob, threatened it royally, and uttered commands that were fun to laugh at, he had been very entertaining. But when weariness silenced him, his tormentors grew bored and sought amusement elsewhere.

He could not recognize his surroundings. He was in London; that was all he knew. He moved on aimlessly. In a little while the houses thinned out and the passersby were infrequent. He washed his bleeding feet in a brook. He rested a few moments, then went on to a large area with only a few scattered houses and a gigantic church, which he recognized. It was covered with scaffolding and swarms of workmen because it was undergoing elaborate repairs. The prince took heart; he felt that his troubles were over now. He thought, "It is the ancient Grey Friars' church, which the king my father has taken from the monks and given to poor children for their home and renamed Christ's Church. They gladly will serve the son of the man who has been so generous to them, especially since that son is as poor and pitiful as anyone who ever has stayed here."

He soon was in the middle of a crowd of boys who were running, jumping, playing ball and leap frog, and generally being noisy. They all were dressed alike, in clothes similar to servants' uniforms. Each wore a saucer-size black cap, which was too small and plain to be useful as a covering or ornament. Their hair fell unparted to the middle of their forehead and was cropped straight around. Each wore a clerical band at the neck; a long, fitted blue gown with full sleeves; a broad red belt; bright yellow stockings; and low shoes with large metal buckles. It was an ugly outfit.

The boys stopped playing and flocked around the prince, who proudly said, "Good lads, tell your master that Edward Prince of Wales wants to speak with him."

A great shout went up at this, and one rude fellow said, "Indeed, are you his grace's messenger, beggar?"

The prince's face flushed with anger, and his hand flew to his hip, but there was nothing there.

A storm of laughter followed, and one boy said, "Did you see that? He fancied that he had a sword, as though he were the prince." This attack brought more laughter.

Edward drew himself up proudly and said, "I *am* the prince, and to insult me while you live on my father's charity reflects badly on you."

This was greatly enjoyed, as the laughter proved. The youth who had first spoken shouted to his comrades, "Ho, swine, slaves, servants of his grace's princely father, where are your manners? Kneel down and show reverence to his kingly presence." With loud laughter they dropped to their knees and pretended to worship the prince.

The prince kicked the nearest boy and said fiercely, "Take that until tomorrow, when I build you a hanging post."

This was going beyond fun. The laughter instantly stopped, and fury took its place. A dozen boys shouted, "Grab him! To the horse pond! To the horse pond! Where are the dogs? Ho there, Lion! Ho, Fangs!" Then followed something that England never had seen before: the sacred heir to the throne was grabbed by common hands and set upon by dogs.

As daylight faded, the prince found himself deep in the city's crowded portion. His body was bruised, his hands were bleeding, and his rags were dirty with mud. He wandered on and on and grew more and more bewildered, and so tired that he hardly could drag one foot after the other. He had stopped asking questions of anyone because they brought him insults instead of information. He kept thinking, "Offal Court. That is the name. If I can find it before my strength is gone and I drop, then I am saved. His people will take me to the palace and prove that I am not theirs but the true prince, and I will reclaim my life." Now and then he thought of his treatment by those rude Christ's Church boys, and he vowed, "When I am king, they will have not only bread and shelter but also education. A full belly is worth little when the mind and heart are starved. I will be sure to remember this as a lesson. Learning softens the heart and encourages gentleness and charity." Lights began to twinkle as a windy, rainy, chilly night set in. The homeless heir to England's throne walked on, drifting deeper into the maze of filthy alleys full of poverty and misery.

Suddenly a large drunken thug seized him and said, "Out 'til this time of night again, and you haven't brought a farthing home, I'm sure. If that's true, I'll break all the bones in your lean body, as sure as I'm John Canty."

The prince twisted himself loose, unconsciously brushed the shoulder that Canty had grabbed, and eagerly said, "Oh, are you his father? Heaven let it be so. Then, you will return me and take him away."

"His father? What do you mean? I know I am *your* father, as you soon will..."

"Oh, no more jokes and delays. I am worn, I am wounded, and I can bear no more. Take me to the king my father, and he will make you rich beyond your wildest dreams. Believe me, man, believe me. I speak the truth. Do what you must to save me. I am the Prince of Wales."

Amazed, the man stared down at the lad, then shook his head and muttered, "He's gone mad."

Then he grabbed him again and said with a rough laugh and a curse, "Mad or not, your Grandma Canty and I soon will find the soft places in your bones, or I'm no true man."

With this, he dragged the frantic and struggling prince away and disappeared up a street, followed by a delighted and noisy crowd.

CHAPTER 5

Tom as Royalty

Left alone in the prince's apartment, Tom Canty made good use of his opportunity. He turned this way and that before the great mirror, admiring his fine clothing. Then he walked away, imitating the prince's elegant posture and watching his reflection. Next he drew the beautiful sword and bowed, kissing the blade and placing it across his chest. Five or six weeks ago he had seen a noble knight do the same thing to salute the Lieutenant of the Tower when delivering the Lord Norfolk and Lord Surrey as prisoners. Tom played with the jeweled dagger that hung at his thigh; he examined the room's costly and beautiful decorations; he tried each of the luxurious chairs and thought how proud he would be if the Offal Court boys could see him like this. He wondered if they would believe the marvelous tale that he would tell when he got home, or if they would shake their heads and say that his imagination had run away with him.

At the end of half an hour, it occurred to Tom that the prince had been gone a long time. He immediately began to feel lonely, and he stopped looking at the riches around him. He grew uneasy, then restless, then upset. Suppose someone came and caught him in the prince's clothes. Without the prince to explain, wouldn't they hang him at once and investigate the situation afterward? He had heard that the nobility made small decisions quickly. Trembling with fear, he softly opened the door to the hallway, planning to find the prince, who would sort everything out. Six well-dressed footmen and two young attendants, dressed like butterflies, sprang to their feet and bowed low before him. He stepped back quickly and shut the door. "Oh, they make fun of me," he thought. "They will go and tell. Why did I come here to throw away my life?" He walked up and down the floor, filled with fear, listening, starting at every little noise.

Soon the door swung open and a polite page announced, "Lady Jane Grey." The door closed, and a sweet young girl, richly dressed, bounded toward him. But she stopped suddenly and asked in a worried voice, "Oh, what troubles you, my lord?"

Tom felt as if he couldn't breathe, but he managed to stammer, "Be merciful! I am no lord but only poor Tom Canty of Offal Court in the city. Please let me see the prince. He will give me back my rags and let me leave unhurt. Oh, be merciful and save me!" By this time the boy was on his knees, pleading not only with his words but also with his eyes and uplifted hands.

The young girl seemed horrified. She cried

out, "Oh, my lord! On your knees? In front of me?" Then she fled in fright.

Weak with despair, Tom sank down, murmuring, "There is no help; there is no hope. Now they will come and take me."

While he lay there numb with terror, terrible news was speeding through the palace. The whispered gossip flew from servant to servant, from lord to lady, down long hallways, from floor to floor, from room to room: "The prince has gone mad! The prince has gone mad!" Soon every room and marble hall was filled with groups of glittering lords, ladies, and lesser folk whispering excitedly, their faces filled with disbelief.

A grand official came marching by these groups, proclaiming, "In the name of the king, let no one believe this false and foolish rumor, on pain of death, nor discuss it with anyone. In the name of the king!" The whisperings stopped as though people suddenly had lost their voices. Soon there was a general buzz along the halls: "The prince! See, the prince comes."

Tom slowly walked past the low-bowing groups, trying to bow in return and meekly looking at his strange surroundings with bewildered and pathetic eyes. Great nobles walked on both sides of him, supporting him to steady his steps. Behind him followed the court doctors and some servants.

Then Tom found himself in a grand apartment of the palace and heard the door close behind him.

Around him stood those who had come with him.

Before him reclined a very large and fat man with a wide, spongy face and a stern expression. His large head was gray; his whiskers, which he wore only around his face, like a frame, also were gray. His clothing was fancy but old and slightly frayed in places. One of his swollen legs had a pillow under it and was wrapped in bandages. There was silence now. Everyone except this man had bent their head in reverence. This stern-faced, sickly man was the dreaded Henry the Eighth. With increasing gentleness in his face, he asked, "How now, my Lord Edward, my prince? Have you been trying to trick me, the good king your father, who loves you and treats you kindly, with a bad joke?"

Tom was listening, as well as his dazed mind would let him, to this speech's beginning. But when he heard the words "me, the good king," his face paled and he dropped to his knees as if he had been shot. Lifting up his hands, he exclaimed, "You are the king? Then, I am ruined indeed!"

This speech stunned the king. His eyes wandered from face to face, then rested, bewildered, on the boy before him. He said in a tone of deep disappointment, "Alas, I had thought that the rumor was false." He sighed deeply and said gently, "Come to your father, child. You are not well."

Tom was assisted to his feet and, humble and trembling, approached the majesty of England.

The king took the frightened face in his hands

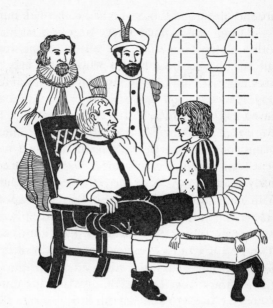

and gazed earnestly and lovingly into it awhile, as
if looking for evidence of sanity. Then he pressed
the curly head against his breast and patted it tenderly. "Do you know your father, child?" he asked.
Do not break my old heart. Say that you know me.
You do know me, yes?"

"Yes, you are my respected lord the king,
whom God will protect."

"True, true. That is right. Be comforted, and
do not tremble. There is no one here who will
hurt you. Everyone here loves you. You are better
now; it was just a bad spell. And you know who
you are now, yes? You will not call yourself by

another name again, as they say you did before?"

"I beg you to believe me. I spoke the truth, most mighty lord. I am the lowest among your subjects, having been born a pauper. It is only an accident that I am here and not my fault. I am too young to die. You can save me with one little word. Oh, speak it, sir!"

"Die? Do not talk like that, sweet prince. Calm your troubled heart. You will not die."

Tom dropped to his knees with a glad cry. "May God reward your mercy, oh my king, and give you a long and happy life!" Springing up, he turned a joyful face toward the two lords in waiting and exclaimed, "You heard it! I am not to die. The king has said it." Everyone bowed in silence. Tom hesitated, a little confused, then turned timidly toward the king, asking, "May I go now?"

"Go? Surely, if you like. But why not stay a little longer? Where would you go?"

Tom dropped his eyes and answered humbly. "Perhaps I misunderstood. I thought that I was free, so I planned to go back to the house where I was born and raised in misery. My mother and sisters live there, so it is my home, whereas these riches that I am not used to... Oh please, sir, let me go!"

The king was silent and thoughtful awhile, and his face revealed a growing distress. Now he said, with a little hope in his voice, "Maybe he is insane only about this one thing, and he still can think normally about other subjects. God let it be so. We will perform a test." Then he asked Tom a question in Latin, and Tom answered him poorly in the same language. The king was delighted and showed it. The lords and doctors also looked pleased. The king said, "It was below his usual level, but it shows that his mind is only diseased, not fatally injured. What do you think, sir?"

The doctor to whom he spoke bowed low and replied, "I agree with you, sire. Your conclusion is correct."

The king looked pleased with this encouragement because it came from a knowledgeable person, and he continued cheerfully, "Everyone, pay attention. We will test him further." He put a question to Tom in French.

Tom stood silent a moment, embarrassed by having so many eyes on him. Then he said shyly, "I do not know this language, your majesty."

The king fell back on his couch. The attendants flew to his side, but he waved them off and said, "Do not bother me. It is only an annoying faintness. Raise me. There, that's enough. Come here, child. Rest your poor troubled head on your father's heart, and be at peace. You soon will be well. It's only a passing fantasy. Do not fear; you will soon be well." Then he turned toward the crowd with a fierce look in his eyes. "Listen, everyone," he said. "My son is mad, but it is not permanent. This is the result of too much studying and time indoors. Away with his books and teachers! See to it. Entertain him with sports and other wholesome activities, so that his health returns."

He raised himself higher and went on with energy. "He is mad, but he is my son and England's heir. Mad or sane, he will rule. Anyone who talks about his condition destroys England's peace and order and will be put to death. Get me a drink; I am thirsty. This sorrow drains my strength... There, take away the cup. Support me. That is better. Mad, is he? If he were a thousand times madder, he still would be Prince of Wales, and I the king will confirm it. Tomorrow he will be appointed officially, with the traditional ceremony. Prepare for it, my Lord Hertford."

One of the nobles knelt at the royal couch and said, "The king's majesty knows that the Hereditary Great Marshal of England lies imprisoned in the Tower. A prisoner cannot..."

"Peace! Do not insult my ears with his hated name. Is this man to live forever? Am I to be denied my wish? Is the prince to wait for his appointment because the realm lacks a loyal earl marshal to invest him with his honors? No, by God's splendor. Tell my parliament to order Norfolk's execution before sunrise, or they will pay dearly."

Lord Hertford said, "The king's will is law," and returned to his usual place.

Gradually the anger faded out of the old king's face and he said, "Kiss me, my prince. There. What are you afraid of? Am I not your loving father?"

"I am unworthy of your kindness, mighty and

gracious lord. But... But it saddens me to think of the prisoner who is going to die, and..."

"Ah, this is just like you. Your heart is the same, even though your mind has suffered; you always were gentle. But this duke stands between you and your honors. I will appoint another marshal to perform his duties. Do not worry about this matter."

"Is it my fault that he must die now, my king? How long might he live otherwise?"

"Do not think about him, my prince. He is unworthy. Kiss me again, and go play your games. I am feeling ill, and I want to rest. Go with your Uncle Hertford and your servants, and come back when I am feeling better."

Tom left with a heavy heart because this last sentence destroyed his hope of being set free. Again he heard the buzz of low voices exclaiming, "The prince! The prince comes." His spirits sank lower and lower as he walked past the glittering rows of bowing attendants. He realized that he was a captive now, and if God did not take pity on him and set him free, he might remain shut up in this golden cage forever, a miserable and friendless prince.

Wherever he looked he seemed to see floating in the air the severed head and familiar face of the great Duke of Norfolk, the eyes fixed on him disapprovingly.

His old dreams had been so pleasant, but this reality was so grim.

CHAPTER 6

Tom Receives Instructions

Tom was conducted to a noble suite's main room and asked to sit down. This made him uncomfortable because there were older, high-ranking men in his presence. He begged them to be seated also, but they only bowed and remained standing. He would have insisted, but his "uncle," the Earl of Hertford, whispered into his ear, "Please do not insist, my lord. It is wrong for them to sit in your presence."

Lord St. John was announced. After paying his respects to Tom, he said, "I am here on behalf of the king, concerning a private matter. Will it please your royal highness to dismiss your attendants, except my lord the Earl of Hertford?"

Seeing that Tom did not know what to do, Hertford whispered that he should make a sign with his hand and not bother to speak unless he chose. When the attendants had left, Lord St. John said, "His majesty commands that, for the nation's security, the prince will hide his illness as much as possible until he regains his health. He will not deny that he is the true prince and heir to

England's throne, and he will behave accordingly. He will not speak of the poor background that he has imagined for himself as a result of his illness. He will try to recognize the people around him, and if he cannot, he will pretend that he does. Whenever he cannot remember the proper thing to say or do, he will not reveal his confusion. Instead he will ask Lord Hertford or the king himself for advice. The king sends greetings to the prince and prays for his quick recovery." Lord St. John bowed and stood aside.

Tom reluctantly replied, "The king has said it. No one may defy the king's order or twist his orders to suit their needs. The king will be obeyed."

Lord Hertford said, "Because the king has forbidden your highness to study, you may wish to pass the time with some light entertainment before going to the banquet."

Tom looked surprised, and he blushed when he saw Lord St. John's sad expression. His lordship said, "Your memory still fails, and your face shows surprise. Do not worry; your health soon will improve. My Lord Hertford speaks of the city's banquet, which two months ago the king requested your highness to attend. Do you recall it now?"

"I am sorry to confess it had slipped my mind," Tom said in a hesitating voice, blushing again.

At that moment Lady Elizabeth and Lady

Jane Grey were announced. The two lords exchanged significant glances, and Hertford stepped quickly toward the door. As the young girls passed him, he said in a low voice, "Ladies, I request that you act naturally and show no surprise at the prince's condition. He hardly can remember a thing."

Meanwhile Lord St. John said into Tom's ear, "Please, sir, keep in mind his majesty's desire. Remember all that you can, and pretend to remember the rest. Do not let your childhood friends know that you have changed. This would hurt them deeply because they love you tenderly. Would you like me to remain, sir? And your uncle?"

Tom indicated his agreement with a gesture and a murmured word because he already was learning and he wanted to do his best to obey the king.

Despite every precaution, the conversation among the young people became a little embarrassing at times. More than once, Tom came close to breaking down and confessing that he could not continue. But Princess Elizabeth or one of the lords always said the right thing to calm him. Once, little Lady Jane turned to Tom and alarmed him with this question: "Have you paid your respects to the queen today, my lord?"

Tom hesitated, looked distressed, and was about to stammer something at random. But Lord St. John jumped in and answered for him with the easy grace of someone used to handling delicate matters. "He has indeed, madam, and she cheered his mood. Isn't that right, your highness?"

Tom mumbled something in agreement but felt that he was on dangerous ground.

Somewhat later it was mentioned that Tom was not allowed to study for the time being. Her little ladyship exclaimed, "It's a pity, such a pity! You were doing well. Have patience. It will not be for long. You will become as learned as your father, able to speak many languages."

"My father!" Tom cried, momentarily off guard. "He hardly can speak well enough to communicate with pigs. And as for being educated..." He looked up and encountered a solemn warning in Lord St. John's eyes. He stopped, blushed, then continued low and sadly, "My illness troubles me again, and my mind wanders. I meant the king no disrespect."

"We know it, sir," Princess Elizabeth said, taking her "brother's" hand between her two palms, respectfully but with tenderness. "Do not worry about that. It is not your fault but that of your illness."

"You are a gentle comforter, sweet lady," Tom said gratefully, "and my heart moves me to thank you for it, if I may be so bold."

Once, giddy little Lady Jane fired a simple Greek phrase at Tom. Princess Elizabeth quickly saw the blankness of Tom's face and replied in Greek on his behalf. Then she immediately changed the subject.

For the most part, time wore on pleasantly. Errors and uncertainty grew less and less frequent, and Tom grew more and more at ease, seeing that everyone was so lovingly eager to help him and overlook his mistakes. When it came out that the little ladies were to accompany him to the Lord Mayor's banquet in the evening, his heart gave a bound of relief and delight. He felt that he would not be friendless among that crowd of strangers. An hour earlier the idea of their going with him would have been terrifying.

Tom's guardian angels, the two lords, felt less comfortable during the conversation than the young people. They felt as if they were piloting a great ship through a dangerous channel. They constantly were on the alert because their task was a serious one. Therefore, when the ladies' visit was drawing to a close and Lord Guilford Dudley was announced, they felt not only that Tom had been sufficiently tired out for the present but also that they themselves were not in the best condition to make their anxious voyage all over again. So they respectfully advised Tom to excuse himself, which he was very glad to do.

There was a pause now, a sort of waiting silence that Tom could not understand. He glanced at Lord Hertford, who gave him a sign, but he failed to understand that as well. Elizabeth came to the rescue with her usual easy grace. She made reverence and said, "Have we the permission of the prince, my brother, to go?"

Tom said, "Indeed, your ladyships can have whatever you wish, although I would rather give you anything but permission to take away your blessed presence. Go safely, and may God be with you." Then he smiled inwardly at the thought, "It's not for nothing that I have lived among princes in my reading, That has taught me how to use their fancy and gracious speech."

When the famous maidens were gone, Tom turned wearily to his keepers and said, "May it please your lordships to let me go into some corner and rest."

Lord Hertford said, "So please your highness. It is for you to command; it is for us to obey. It is a good idea for you to rest because you must travel to the city soon." He touched a bell and a page appeared, who was ordered to bring Sir William Herbert. This gentleman came immediately and brought Tom to an inner apartment.

Tom's first movement there was to reach for a cup of water. But a silk-and-velvet servant seized it, dropped to one knee, and offered it to him on a gold tray. Next the tired captive sat down and was going to take off his boots. He timidly asked permission with his eyes, but another servant went down onto his knees and took over the task. Tom tried a few more times to help himself, but being promptly prevented each time, he finally gave up, with a sigh of resignation and a murmured "It is a wonder that they do not also try to breathe for me."

Wearing slippers and a luxurious robe, he finally lay down to rest. But he didn't sleep. His head was too full of thoughts and the room too full of people. He could not dismiss the thoughts, so they stayed. He did not know enough to dismiss the people, so they stayed as well, to his regret and theirs.

Tom's departure had left his two noble guardians alone. They mused awhile, with much head shaking and walking the floor. Then Lord St. John said, "Honestly, what do you think?"

"The king is near his end, my nephew is mad, he will mount the throne mad, and he will remain mad. God protect England because she will need it."

"Indeed, that is how it looks. Have you no misgivings about... about...?" The speaker hesitated and finally stopped. He evidently felt that he was on delicate ground.

Lord Hertford stopped before him, looked into his face with clear, honest eyes, and said, "Speak on. There is no one except me to hear. Misgivings about what?"

"I am reluctant to say what is on my mind, with you so closely related to him, my lord. But with all due respect, does it not seem strange that madness could so change his posture and manner? His behavior and speech still are princely, but they are different than before. Is it not strange that madness would make him forget his father's face, royal customs, and, leaving him his Latin, strip him of his Greek and French? My lord, don't be offended, but ease my mind of worry and receive my grateful thanks. It haunts me, his saying that he was not the prince, and so..."

"Peace, my lord. You speak treason. Have you forgotten the king's command? Remember, I am party to your crime if I even listen."

St. John paled and hurried to say, "I was wrong. Do not betray me. Grant me this favor out of your courtesy, and I will neither think nor speak of this thing again. If you deal harshly with me, sir, I will be ruined."

"I am content, my lord. If you do not speak wrongly again, to me or to others, I will act as though you never said anything. You do not need to have misgivings. He is my sister's son. Are not his voice, face, and body familiar to me since he was in his cradle? Madness can do all the strange and confusing things you see in him, and more. Do you remember how old Baron Marley, being mad, forgot his own face, which he had known for sixty years, and said it was another's? He even claimed that he was Mary Magdalene's son and that his head was made of Spanish glass. He would let no one touch it for fear that it would shatter. Do not worry, my lord. This is the true prince; I know him well. Soon he will be your king. You should think about that instead of your other worries."

They talked some more. Lord St. John covered up his mistake as well as he could by repeated protests that his faith was strong now and could not be weakened by doubts again.

Then Lord Hertford relieved his colleague and sat down to keep watch alone. He soon was deep in meditation. The longer he thought, the more he was bothered. After a while he began to pace the floor and mutter. "Tsk, he *must* be the prince. Will anyone in all the land argue that there can be two, not of one blood and birth, so marvelously alike? Even if it were so, it would be an even stranger miracle if chance put the one into the other's place. No, it's folly." He reasoned, "If he were an impostor and called himself a prince, it would be natural. But was there ever an impostor who, being called prince by the king, by the court, by all, denied his dignity and pleaded *against* his adoration? No. By the soul of St. Swithin, no. This is the true prince, gone mad."

CHAPTER 7

Tom's First Royal Dinner

Some time after one in the afternoon, Tom resignedly underwent the ordeal of being dressed for dinner. He found himself as finely clothed as before, but everything was changed, from his collar to his stockings.

He then was brought with much ceremony to a spacious and ornate apartment, where a table was set for one. The apartment's furniture was of heavy gold beautified with designs by the famous artist Benvenuto, which made it priceless. The room was half filled with noble servants.

A chaplain said grace, and Tom was about to start eating because he was not used to waiting when food was available. He was interrupted by the Earl of Berkeley, who fastened a napkin around his neck. Members of this noble's family always had served as Diaperers to the Prince of Wales. Tom's cupbearer was present and stopped all his attempts to help himself to wine. The Taster to his highness the Prince of Wales also was there, prepared to taste any suspicious dish and risk being poisoned. At this time he was largely an ornamental accessory, seldom called on to perform his function; but there had been times, not long ago, when the office of taster had been a dangerous one. It seems strange that they did not use a dog or another animal, but all of royalty's ways are strange. Lord d'Arcy, First Groom of the Chamber, was there, to do goodness knows what. The Lord Chief Butler was there and stood behind Tom's chair overseeing the formalities, under command of the Lord Great Steward and the Lord Head Cook, who stood nearby. Tom had 384 servants besides these; not even a fourth of them were in that room. Tom was not even aware yet that they existed.

All who were present had been drilled within the hour to remember that the prince was temporarily out of his head and to be careful to show no surprise at his changes. These "changes" soon were on display, but this aroused only their compassion and sorrow, not their laughter. It was hard for them to see their beloved prince so ill.

Tom ate with his fingers mainly, but no one smiled at this or even seemed to notice. He inspected his napkin with deep interest because it was of a very dainty and beautiful fabric. Then he said with simplicity, "Please take it away, in case I carelessly get it dirty." The Hereditary Diaperer took it away reverently and without protest.

Tom examined the turnips and the lettuce with interest. He asked what they were and if they were to be eaten. It was only recently that people had begun to raise these things in England instead of importing them as luxuries from Holland. His question was answered with grave respect and without any surprise.

When he had finished his dessert, he filled his pockets with nuts. Nobody appeared to be aware of it or disturbed by it. But the next moment he himself was disturbed because this was the only action he had been permitted to perform with his own hands during the meal. He felt, therefore, that he must have done something most improper and unprincely.

At that moment his nose began to twitch, and the end of it lifted and wrinkled. This continued, and Tom felt more and more distressed. He looked appealingly at one and then another of the lords around him, and tears came into his eyes. They sprang forward with dismay in their faces and begged to know his trouble. Tom said with genuine anguish, "I need your assistance. My nose itches cruelly. What is the custom in this situation? Please hurry because I cannot bear it much longer." No one smiled. Everyone was greatly perplexed and nervously looked at one another for advice. Behold, here was a great wall and nothing in English history to tell how to get over it. The Master of Ceremonies was not present. There was no one who felt safe to sail on this uncharted sea or risk an attempt to solve this serious problem. Alas, there was no Hereditary Scratcher.

Meanwhile the tears had overflowed their banks and begun to trickle down Tom's cheeks. His twitching nose was pleading more urgently than ever for relief. At last, nature broke down the barrier of good manners. Tom said an inward prayer for pardon if he was doing wrong and brought relief to his worried servants by scratching his nose himself.

After his meal a lord brought a shallow gold dish with fragrant rosewater, with which to clean his mouth and fingers. The Hereditary Diaperer stood by with a napkin for his use. Tom gazed at the dish a puzzled moment or two, then raised it to his lips and gravely took a drink. Then he returned it to the waiting lord and remarked, "I don't like it, my lord. It has a pretty flavor but no strength." This new strangeness of the prince's ruined mind made all the hearts around him ache.

Tom's next unconscious blunder was to get up and leave the table just when the chaplain had taken his stand behind his chair and, with uplifted hands and closed eyes, was starting the blessing. Still, nobody seemed to notice that the prince had done anything unusual.

By his own request, our small friend now was taken to his private apartment and left there alone. Hanging on hooks in the oak wall were several pieces of a suit of shining steel armor covered with beautiful gold designs. This armor belonged to the true prince. It was a recent present from Madam Parr, the queen. Tom put on the lower legs, the gloves, the plumed helmet, and the other pieces that he could put on without assistance. For a while he wanted to call for help and complete the matter. But then he thought about the nuts that he had brought from dinner and the joy that it would be to eat them with no one to watch and no Grand Hereditaries to pester him with undesired services. So he restored the pretty things to their places and soon was cracking nuts, feeling almost happy for the first time since God had punished him by making him a prince.

When the nuts all were gone, he stumbled across some inviting books in a closet, including one about the customs of the English court. This was a prize. He lay down on a luxurious couch and proceeded to instruct himself with enthusiasm.

CHAPTER 8

The Question of the Seal

About five o'clock, Henry the Eighth awoke from an unrefreshing nap and thought, "Troubling dreams, troubling dreams. My end is at hand, these warnings say, and my failing pulse confirms it." A wicked light flamed in his eye, and he muttered, "I will not die until he goes first."

Seeing that he was awake, one of his attendants asked if he would see the Lord Chancellor, who was waiting outside.

"Admit him! Admit him!" the king eagerly exclaimed.

The Lord Chancellor entered and knelt by the king's couch, saying, "I have given orders. According to the king's command, the nobles are waiting in the parliament. They have confirmed the Duke of Norfolk's doom, and they humbly await his majesty's wish in the matter."

The king's face lit up with fierce joy. "Lift me up," he said. I myself will go before the parliament. With my own hand I will seal the warrant that will rid me of..." His voice failed and an ashen paleness swept the flush from his cheeks. The attendants eased him back on his pillows and hurriedly assisted him with medicine. Then he said sorrowfully, "Alas, how I have longed for this sweet hour. It comes too late, and I am robbed of what I most desire. Hurry! Let others do this great honor because I cannot. I ask you to act for me. Choose the lords who will carry out my wishes, and get to work. Hurry, man! Before the sun rises and sets again, bring me his head."

"It will be done according to the king's command. Will your majesty give me the Seal, so that I can start this business?"

"The Seal? Who keeps the Seal but you?"

"Please your majesty, you took it from me two days ago, saying that you wanted to use it yourself on the Duke of Norfolk's warrant."

"Why, so I did. I remember. What did I do with it? I am very feeble. So often these days my memory plays tricks on me. It's strange, strange..." The king dropped into inarticulate mumblings, shaking his gray head weakly from time to time and trying to recollect what he had done with the Seal.

At last Lord Hertford knelt and offered information. "Sire, if I may be so bold, several of us remember that you gave the Great Seal to his highness the Prince of Wales until the day that..."

"True, true," the king interrupted. "Fetch it. Go! Time flies."

Lord Hertford flew to Tom but returned to

the king before very long, troubled and empty-handed. He reported, "It grieves me, my lord the king, to bring such unwelcome news. It is God's will that the prince's condition still holds him, and he cannot remember that he received the Seal. I came back quickly to report this, thinking that it would waste precious time to search the many chambers and rooms that belong to his royal high..."

A groan from the king interrupted the lord. His majesty said sadly, "Trouble him no more, poor child. The hand of God lies heavy on him. My heart goes out in loving compassion for him and sorrow that I may not bear his burden on my own old, trouble-weighted shoulders and so bring him peace." He closed his eyes, fell to mumbling, and then was silent.

After a time he opened his eyes again and gazed vacantly around until he saw the kneeling Lord Chancellor. Instantly his face flushed with wrath. "What, you are still here? By God's glory, if you do not see to that traitor's execution, your hat will have a vacation tomorrow because it will have no head to sit on."

The trembling chancellor answered, "Your majesty, I beg your mercy! I wait for the Seal."

"Man, have you lost your wits? The small seal that I used to take abroad lies in my treasury. Because the Great Seal has flown away, the small one will suffice. Have you lost your wits? Be gone! And listen: come no more until you bring his head."

The chancellor did not delay, and the commission immediately commanded the parliament to do its work. The next day, England's highest noble, the Duke of Norfolk, would be beheaded.

CHAPTER 9

The River Pageant

At nine in the evening the palace's whole vast riverfront was ablaze with light. The river itself was so thickly covered with fishing boats and pleasure barges, all fringed with colored lanterns, that it resembled a limitless, glowing garden of flowers moving in the summer wind. Large enough for an army, the grand terrace of stone steps leading down to the water was a picture to see, with royal guards in polished armor and troops of brilliantly costumed servants bustling around.

A command was given, and immediately all living creatures vanished from the steps. The air was heavy with the hush of suspense. In the boats, crowds of people rose, shaded their eyes from the glare of lanterns and torches, and gazed toward the palace.

A row of forty or fifty official barges drew up to the steps. They were covered with gold, and their high prows and sterns were elaborately carved. Some of them were decorated with banners and streamers, some with gold cloth and tapestries embroidered with coats of arms. Others had silk flags with little silver bells that shook out tiny

showers of joyous music whenever the breeze
blew. Belonging to nobles who served the prince,
the more magnificent barges wore shields embla-
zoned with coats of arms. Each official barge was
towed by a small boat. Besides the rowers, these
boats carried guards in glossy armor and a company of musicians.

The front of the procession now appeared in
the great gateway. The troop of sentries was
dressed in black-and-brown striped stockings; velvet caps with silver roses; and purple-and-blue
jackets with the prince's symbol, three feathers,
embroidered in gold on the front and back. Their
ax-head spears were covered with red velvet and
decorated with gold tassels. Filing off to the right
and left, they formed two long lines extending
from the palace's gateway to the water's edge. A
thick carpet was unfolded between them by attendants wearing the gold-and-crimson uniforms of
the prince.

Then trumpets blasted from within the palace.
A lively prelude arose from the musicians on the
water, and two ushers with white wands marched
with a slow and stately pace from the gate. They
were followed by one officer bearing the govern-
ment staff and another carrying the city's sword.
Next came several sergeants of the city guard in
full uniform; the garter king-at-arms in his official
coat; several knights of the bath, each with white
lace on their sleeves; their attendants; judges in
scarlet caps and robes; England's Lord High

Chancellor in a scarlet robe; legislators in scarlet cloaks; and the heads of various civic companies in robes of state. Now came twelve gentlemen of the French ambassador's office in splendid white-and-gold costumes, with collars of crimson velvet lined with violet taffeta. They made their way down the steps, followed by twelve knights of the Spanish ambassador clothed in black velvet without any decoration. Following these came several great English nobles with their attendants.

Another flourish of trumpets announced the appearance of the prince's uncle, the future Duke of Somerset, who emerged from the gateway. He was dressed in a shiny black tunic and a crimson satin cloak flowered with gold and edged with silver ribbon. He turned, removed his plumed cap, bent his body in reverence, and began to step backward, bowing at each step.

A prolonged trumpet blast followed and the proclamation "Make way for the high and mighty Lord Edward, Prince of Wales!" Atop the palace walls a long line of flame leaped forth with a thunder crash. The crowd on the river burst into a roar of welcome. Tom Canty, the cause and hero of it all, stepped into view and slightly bowed his princely head. He was magnificently dressed in a white satin tunic edged with white fur and decorated, at the chest, with purple cloth sprinkled with diamonds. Over this he wore a white cloak decorated with a triple-feather pattern, set with pearls and precious stones, lined with blue satin,

and fastened with a clasp of diamonds. Around his neck hung the emblem of the garter and several princely foreign emblems. Wherever light fell on him, jewels responded with a blinding flash. Oh, thought Tom Canty, born in a shack, bred in London's gutters, familiar with rags and dirt and misery, "what a spectacle this is!"

CHAPTER 10

The Prince in Offal Court

We left John Canty dragging the rightful prince into Offal Court, with a noisy and delighted mob at his heels. Only one person pleaded for the captive, and he hardly was heard. The prince continued to struggle for freedom and to rage against his harsh treatment until Canty lost what little patience was left in him and raised his oak club over the prince's head in fury. The single pleader sprang to intervene, and the blow descended on his wrist. Canty roared, "You meddle, do you? Then, have your reward." His club crashed down on the meddler's head. The man groaned and sank to the ground amid the crowd's feet. The next moment he lay there alone in the dark. The mob had pressed on, undisturbed by the episode.

Soon the prince found himself in John Canty's house, with the door closed. By the dim light of a candle in a bottle, he saw his dismal surroundings and also its occupants. Two messy girls and a middle-aged woman cowered in one corner, like tortured animals who expected more abuse. From another corner came a withered hag with gray hair and evil eyes. John Canty said to her, "Wait. There is treasure here. Do nothing until you've heard. Then let your hand be as heavy as you like. Come here, lad. Now say your ridiculous things again, if you haven't forgotten. Say your name. Who are you?"

The prince blushed at the insult. He gave Canty a steady, indignant look and said, "You show your bad upbringing by commanding me to speak. I tell you now, as I told you before, that I am Edward, Prince of Wales."

The stunning surprise of this reply nailed the hag's feet to the floor where she stood and almost took her breath away. She stared at the prince in stupid amazement, which so amused her criminal son that he burst into a roar of laughter.

The effect on Tom Canty's mother and sisters was different. Their fear of bodily injury immediately gave way to distress of a different sort. Looking dismayed, they ran forward exclaiming, "Oh, poor Tom! Poor lad." The mother fell to her knees before the prince, put her hands on his shoulders, and gazed into his face through her rising tears. "Oh, my poor boy," she said. "Your foolish reading has taken your senses. Ah! Why did you keep reading after I warned you about it? You have broken your mother's heart."

The prince looked into her face and said gently, "Your son is well and has not lost his wits, good dame. Do not worry. Take me to the palace where he is, and the king, my father, will give him back to you."

"The king, your father! Oh, my child. Do not say such awful things. Come out of this horrible dream, and take back your memory. Look at me. Am I not your mother, who loves you?"

The prince shook his head and reluctantly said, "God knows, I do not want to hurt you, but truly I never have seen you before."

The woman sat back on the floor and, covering her eyes with her hands, gave way to heartbroken sobs and wailings.

"Let the show go on!" Canty shouted. "Nan! Bet! Rude wenches, will you stand in the prince's presence? On your knees, pauper scum, and show him reverence." He followed this with another coarse laugh.

The girls began to plead timidly for their brother. "If you just will let him go to bed, a good night's sleep will cure his madness," Nan said. "Please let him go."

"Do, father," Bet said. "He is worn out. Tomorrow he will be himself again and will beg well. He will not come home empty-handed again."

This remark turned Canty serious and brought his mind to business. He angrily turned on the prince and said, "Tomorrow we must pay two pennies to the landlord. We must pay half a year's rent, or out we go. Show what you have gathered with your lazy begging."

The prince said, "Do not offend me with your depressing matters. I tell you again that I am the king's son."

A hard blow on the shoulder from Canty's broad palm sent the prince staggering into Tom's mother, who hugged him, sheltering him with her own body from a pelting rain of blows and slaps. The frightened girls retreated to their corner, but the grandmother eagerly stepped forward to assist her son. The prince sprang away from Tom's mother, exclaiming, "You will not suffer for me, madam. Let these swine hurt me alone."

This speech angered the pair so much that they worked the boy over and then gave the girls and their mother a beating for showing sympathy for him. "Now," Canty said, "to bed, all of you. The entertainment has tired me."

The light was put out, and the family retired. As soon as John Canty and his mother were snoring, the young girls crept to where the prince lay and tenderly covered him with straw and rags. Their mother crept to him too, stroked his hair, and cried over him while whispering broken words of comfort and compassion. She had saved a morsel for him to eat, but the boy's pain had destroyed his appetite, at least for black and tasteless crusts. He was touched by her brave and painful defense of him and by her comfort. He thanked her in noble and princely words and begged her to go to sleep and try to forget her sorrows. He added that the king his father would not let her loyal kindness and devotion go unrewarded. This return to his "madness" broke her heart again, and she repeatedly hugged him. Then, drowned in tears, she returned to her bed.

As she lay thinking and crying, the idea that something about this boy was not like Tom, mad or sane, crept into her mind. She could not tell just what it was, but her sharp mother-instinct detected it. What if the boy really wasn't her son? Oh, absurd! She almost smiled at the idea, despite her grief and troubles. But the idea persisted. It pursued her, clung to her, and refused to go away. At last she realized that she would have no peace of mind until she invented a test to determine whether this lad was her son. Yes, this plainly was the thing to do. She considered one possible test after another but rejected all of them. None of them was perfect, and an imperfect test could not satisfy her. It seemed pointless to keep trying.

Her ear caught the boy's regular breathing, and she knew that he had fallen asleep. While she listened, his measured breathing was broken by a soft, startled cry such as one utters during a troubling dream. This gave her an idea that was better than all her previous ones combined. As she started to relight her candle, she thought, "If I had seen him just then, I would have known. Ever since that day long ago when the powder burst in his face, he always has put up his hands after being startled out of his sleep or thoughts. He doesn't do it as other people do, with the palm inward, but always with the palm turned outward. I have seen him do it a hundred times, always the same way. Yes, I soon will know."

With the candle shaded in her hand, she crept

to the slumbering boy's side. Scarcely breathing, she bent over him and suddenly flashed the light in his face and struck the floor by his ear with her knuckles. The sleeper's eyes sprang open and he looked around with alarm, but he made no special movement with his hands.

The poor woman was smitten with surprise and grief, but she managed to hide her emotions. She soothed the boy to sleep again, then crept off to lament her experiment's disastrous result. She tried to believe that Tom's madness had made his special gesture disappear, but she could not. "No," she thought, "his hands are not mad; they could not unlearn such an old habit so quickly. This is a heavy day for me."

Still, she could not bring herself to accept the outcome, which could have been an accident. She must test him again. So she startled the boy out of his sleep a second and a third time, with the same results as before. Sorrowful, she dragged herself to bed and fell asleep, thinking, "But I cannot give him up. No, I cannot. He *must* be my boy."

The prince now fell into a deep sleep. Four or five hours later his slumber began to lighten. Half asleep and half awake, he murmured, "Sir William! Ho, Sir William Herbert! Come here, and listen to the strangest dream that ever... Sir William! Are you listening, man? I thought I had changed into a pauper, and.... Ho there! Guards! Sir William! What? Is there no groom of the chamber in waiting? Alas, it will go hard with..."

"What is wrong with you?" Nan whispered to him. "Who are you calling?"

"Sir William Herbert. Who are *you*?"

"I? Who *would* I be but your sister Nan? Oh, Tom, I forgot. You still are mad, poor boy. I wish I never had awakened again. Please keep quiet, or we'll be beaten to death."

The startled prince sprang partly up but got a sharp reminder from his stiffened bruises. With a moan, he sank back onto his foul straw. "Alas, it was no dream, then." In a moment he felt all the heavy sorrow and misery that sleep had erased. He realized that he no longer was a spoiled prince in a palace, with a nation's adoring eyes on him, but a pauper, an outcast in rags, a prisoner in a cave fit only for beasts, among beggars and thieves. In the midst of his grief he heard shouting a block or two away.

The next moment there were several sharp raps at the door. John Canty stopped snoring and asked, "Who knocks? What do you want?"

A voice answered, "Do you know who you clubbed last night?"

"No, and I don't care."

"You'll soon wish you did. If you want to live, you must flee. The man is now on his deathbed. It's the priest, Father Andrew."

"God have mercy!" Canty exclaimed. He roused his family and hoarsely commanded, "Go now, or stay here and perish."

Scarcely five minutes later the Cantys were in the street and flying for their lives. John Canty held the prince by the wrist and hurried him along in the dark, warning him in a low voice, "Watch what you say, you mad fool, and don't speak our name. I will choose a new name to throw the law's dogs off the scent. Mind your tongue, I tell you!" He growled these words to the rest of the family: "If we get separated, make for London Bridge. Wait at the last linen draper's shop until everyone comes. Then we will flee into Southwark together."

At this moment the group burst out of darkness into a crowd of singing, dancing, and shouting people on the riverfront. A line of bonfires stretched up and down the Thames, lighting up both London Bridge and Southwark Bridge. The entire river glowed with the flash and sheen of colored lights, and constant fireworks almost turned night into day. Crowds of revelers were everywhere. All of London seemed to be attending.

John Canty cursed furiously and ordered his family to retreat, but it was too late. In an instant they were swallowed up in the swarming crowd and hopelessly separated from one another. But Canty still gripped the prince, whose heart was beating high with hopes of escape. A large drunk waterman found himself rudely shoved by Canty in his efforts to plow through the crowd. He laid his great hand on Canty's shoulder and said, "What's the hurry, friend? Do you busy yourself with serious matters while all loyal subjects are celebrating?"

"My affairs are my own. They don't concern you," Canty answered roughly. "Remove your hand and let me pass."

"Since that is your attitude, you may not leave until you have drunk to the Prince of Wales," the waterman said, barring the way.

"Hurry, give me the cup."

Other revelers were interested. They cried out, "The loving cup! The loving cup! Make the spoilsport drink the loving cup, or we'll feed him to the fishes." So a huge loving cup was brought. Grasping one handle with one of his hands, the waterman formally presented the cup to Canty.

According to ancient custom, Canty had to grasp the opposite handle with one hand and remove the lid with the other. This left the prince free for a second. He immediately dived into the forest of legs around him and disappeared. In another moment he was as hard to find as a coin in the ocean.

He soon forgot about John Canty and realized that the city was honoring a false Prince of Wales. He decided that the pauper lad, Tom Canty, had deliberately taken advantage of an amazing opportunity and become an imposter. Therefore, there was only one thing to do: find his way to the Guildhall, make himself known, and denounce the impostor. He also decided that Tom should be allowed a reasonable time for spiritual preparation before being hanged, drawn, and quartered, according to the law in cases of high treason.

CHAPTER 11

At Guildhall

Attended by its splendid fleet of illuminated boats, the royal barge glided down the Thames. The air was filled with music, and firelight lit the riverbanks. The distant city glowed from countless bonfires, which made the rooftops sparkle like jewels. The moving fleet was greeted from the banks with a continuous hoarse roar of cheers and the constant flash and boom of artillery.

Tom Canty, half buried in his silk cushions, was astonished by this spectacle. However, the little friends at his side, Princess Elizabeth and Lady Jane Grey, were not at all impressed.

At the Dowgate the fleet was towed up the Walbrook channel to Bucklersbury, past houses and under well-lit bridges filled with merrymakers. It halted in a basin in the center of London. Tom disembarked, and he and his gallant procession crossed Cheapside and made a short march through the Old Jewry and Basinghall Street to the Guildhall.

Tom and his little ladies were received with formality by the Lord Mayor and the Fathers of the City, in their scarlet robes and gold chains, and conducted to the head of the great hall. Before they entered, heralds announced their presence, and the City Sword was brought in. The lords and ladies who were to wait on Tom and his two small friends took their places behind their chairs.

The court nobles and other noble guests were seated at a table with the city's business leaders. Lesser citizens took places at a multitude of other tables. From high perches, statues of Gog and Magog, the city's ancient guardians, watched the familiar spectacle below them. There was a bugle blast and a proclamation, and a fat butler appeared, followed by servants bringing a royal hunk of beef, smoking hot and ready for the knife.

After grace, Tom rose, and the whole house stood up with him. He and Princess Elizabeth drank from a large gold goblet, which then passed to Lady Jane and through the assembled crowd. So the banquet began.

By midnight the revelry was at its height. After space was made, a baron and an earl entered, dressed in Turkish costume. They wore long gold robes and red velvet hats; each had two curved swords called scimitars. Next came another baron and another earl, in long Russian gowns of yellow, white, and red satin, wearing gray fur hats and pointed boots. Each held a hatchet. After them came a knight and the Lord High Admiral, accompanied by five nobles in crimson velvet tunics with silver chains, red satin cloaks, and feather hats. The hundred torchbearers wore crimson and green

satin. Minstrels, dressed in disguises, danced wild-
ly. So did the lords and ladies, to everyone's
delight.

While Tom, in his high seat, gazed on this
dancing, lost in the costumes' swirling colors, the
ragged but real Prince of Wales was denouncing
the impostor and demanding admission at
Guildhall's gates. The crowd greatly enjoyed this
episode and craned their necks to see the small
rioter. Soon they began to mock him, taunting
him into a higher, more entertaining fury. Tears of
humiliation sprang to his eyes, but he stood his
ground and royally defied the mob. The mocking
continued, and he exclaimed, "I tell you again,
you pack of rude dogs, I am the Prince of Wales.
Although I am abandoned and friendless, I will
not back down."

"Whether or not you are the prince, you are a
brave boy and not friendless. I stand here by your
side to prove it. You could do a lot worse for a
friend than Miles Hendon. Take a break, my child.
I speak the language of these base kennel rats like
a native." The speaker looked like a poor noble.
He was tall, trim, and muscular. His tunic and
trousers were fine but threadbare, and their gold
lace was worn. His collar was rumpled and damaged; the feather in his slouched hat was broken
and dirty. At his side he wore a long sword in a
rusty iron sheath, and he moved with a swagger.

His speech was received with an explosion of
jeers and laughter. Some cried, "It's another

prince in disguise! Watch out for him; he's dangerous. Yes, he seems it; look at his eyes. Take the
lad from him. To the horse pond with the boy!"
Instantly a hand was laid on the prince. As instantly the stranger's long sword was out, and a thump
from the flat of it felled the meddler. The next
moment a number of voices shouted, "Kill the
dog! Kill him! Kill him!"

The mob closed in on the warrior, who
backed himself against a wall and began to strike

around him, like a madman, with his sword. His victims sprawled this way and that, but the mob kept coming at him with undiminished fury. His destruction seemed certain when a trumpet blast sounded, a voice shouted, "Make way for the king's messenger!" and a troop of horsemen came charging down on the mob. People fled out of the way. The bold stranger grabbed the prince and soon was far from danger and the crowd.

Back in the Guildhall, the revelers continued their celebration. High above the joyous activity, a bugle note sounded. There was instant silence. While the whole audience stood and listened, a palace messenger delivered a proclamation. Its last solemn words were "The king is dead."

The gatherers bowed their heads in deep silence. After a few moments everyone fell to their knees and stretched out their hands towards Tom, and a mighty shout burst forth that seemed to shake the building: "Long live the king!"

Tom's dazed eyes wandered over this spectacle and finally rested on the kneeling princesses beside him. Then he saw the Earl of Hertford. A sudden purpose showed in his face. Softly he said into Lord Hertford's ear, "Answer me honestly. If I gave a command, which no one but a king could issue, would anyone defy it?"

"No one, your highness, in the entire kingdom. You are the authority of England. You are the king. Your word is law."

Tom responded in a strong, earnest voice,

"Then, from now on the king's law will be the law of mercy and never again the law of blood. Up from your knees and away! To the Tower! Say that the king commands that the Duke of Norfolk shall not die."

The words eagerly were carried throughout the hall. As Hertford hurried away, another great shout burst forth: "The reign of blood is ended! Long live Edward, king of England!"

CHAPTER 12

The King and his Deliverer

As soon as Miles Hendon and the new king were free of the mob, they went through back lanes and alleys toward the river. Their way was clear until they approached London Bridge, where they plowed into the crowd again, Hendon keeping a tight grip on the prince's (no, the king's) wrist.

The important news already was out, and the boy learned it from a thousand voices at once. "The king is dead!" The news chilled his heart and made him shudder. He realized the greatness of his loss and was filled with bitter grief because the grim tyrant who had been such a terror to others always had been gentle with him. Tears blurred his vision. For a moment he felt like the most abandoned, outcast, and forgotten of God's creatures. Then another cry shook the night: "Long live King Edward the Sixth!" This made his eyes sparkle and thrilled him with pride. "Ah," he thought, "how grand and strange. I am king."

Our friends slowly threaded their way through the crowds on the Bridge. This structure had stood for six hundred years, and it always had been a busy, noisy road. Each side was lined with shops, and families lived in the rooms above them. The Bridge was, in itself, a sort of town, with its own inn, beerhouses, bakeries, haberdasheries, food markets, manufacturing industries, and church.

Bridge residents saw the two neighbors that it linked—London and Southwark—as fine enough, as suburbs go, but not particularly important. London Bridge was a tight-knit community, with only a single street a fifth of a mile long. Everyone had known one another, and one another's business, for generations. The Bridge had its own aristocracy: fine old families of butchers, bakers, and others who had occupied the same old buildings for five or six hundred years. These families knew the Bridge's entire history and all its legends. They always talked Bridgey talk, thought Bridgey thoughts, and generally were narrow, ignorant, and conceited. Children of Bridge families grew up and died without setting foot anywhere except the Bridge. Such people naturally imagined that life on the Bridge afforded a view of everything that was most important. This attitude was reinforced during a royal procession, when Bridge families commanded a perfect view from their windows high above the street.

People born and raised on London Bridge found life unbearably dull and empty elsewhere. History tells of one man who left the Bridge at the age of seventy-one and retired to the country. Every night, he tossed and turned in his bed, unable to sleep, because the deep stillness was so painful and oppressive. At last, a tired ghost, he fled back to his old home, where—lulled by waves and the Bridge's noise—he fell peacefully asleep.

During this period, the Bridge taught its children lessons in English history by impaling the discolored, decaying heads of famous criminals and traitors on iron spikes atop its gates. But that is another story.

Hendon lived in the Bridge's little inn. As he walked to the door with his small friend, a rough voice said, "So, you have come at last. You will not escape again. Maybe pounding your bones to a pudding can teach you not to keep us waiting." John Canty put out his hand to seize the boy.

Hendon stepped in the way and said, "Not so fast, friend. You are too rough. How do you know this boy?"

"It's none of your business, but he is my son."

"It's a lie!" the little king cried hotly.

"I believe you whether your small head is solid or cracked, my boy. But it doesn't matter whether this bully is your father or not. I will not allow him to beat you if you prefer to stay with me."

"I do. I do. I don't know him. I hate him and will die before I go with him."

"Then, it's settled. There is no more to say."

"We will see about that!" Canty exclaimed, striding past Hendon to get at the boy. "I will make him..."

"If you touch him, you piece of garbage, I will skewer you like a goose," Hendon said, barring the way and putting his hand on his sword hilt. Canty drew back. "Now listen," Hendon continued. "I took this lad under my protection when a mob like you would have beaten him, perhaps killed him. Do you think I will desert him now to a worse fate? Even if you were his father, which I don't believe, a quick death would be more merciful to this boy than a life with you. Go on your way quickly; I am not a patient man."

Canty moved off, muttering threats and curses, and was swallowed by the crowd.

Hendon ordered a meal for his room and took the boy up three flights of stairs to a poor apartment. It had a shabby bed and some odds and ends of old furniture and was dimly lit by two sickly candles.

The little king dragged himself to the bed and lay down on it, exhausted and hungry. He had been on his feet a good part of a day and night and had eaten nothing. He murmured drowsily, "Please call me when the table is set," and immediately sank into a deep sleep.

A smile twinkled in Hendon's eyes, and he thought, "My word, the little beggar comes into one's home and takes over one's bed with a grace as natural as if he owned them, without even asking permission. In his diseased ravings he called himself the Prince of Wales, and he plays the part well. Poor little friendless rat. Doubtless his mind has been ruined by troubles. Well, I will be his friend. I have saved him, and I already love the bold little rascal. How bravely he defied the dirty mob! And what a sweet and gentle face he has while peacefully sleeping. I will teach him and make him healthy. I will be his elder brother and watch over him. Anyone who shames or hurts him will not live long."

He bent over the boy and looked at him kindly, patting the young cheek tenderly and smoothing back the tangled curls with his great brown hand. The boy shivered slightly. Hendon thought, "It is just like a man to let him lie here uncovered and catch cold. Now, what should I do? It will wake him to put him under the covers, and he badly needs to sleep." He looked around for extra blankets but, finding none, took off his jacket and wrapped the boy in it, thinking, "I am used to the cold."

He walked up and down the room to keep warm. "His insanity tells him that he is the Prince of Wales," Hendon pondered. "It will be odd to have a Prince of Wales still with us, now that the prince is king. His poor mind is fixed on one fantasy, and he will not figure out that he should call himself the king... If my father is still alive after these seven years that I have been away, he will welcome the poor lad and give him generous shelter for my sake. So will my good elder brother, Arthur. My other brother, Hugh... If the rude, cruel scoundrel interferes, I will crack his crown. We should go there right away."

A servant entered with a smoking meal, put it on a small table, placed the chairs, and left. The door slammed after him, and the noise woke the boy, who sat up with a happy expression. Then a sad look came over his face, and he murmured with a deep sigh, "Alas, it was only a dream. Woe is me." He noticed Hendon's jacket, realized the sacrifice that had been made for him, and said gently, "You are good to me. Yes, very good. Take it and put it on. I don't need it anymore." He got up and walked to the washstand in the corner and stood there waiting.

Hendon said cheerfully, "We'll have a hearty supper now because everything is savory and smoking hot. Soon you'll feel like a new man."

The boy made no answer but stared in surprise and impatience at the tall knight.

Puzzled, Hendon asked, "What's wrong?"

"Good sir, I want to wash."

"Oh, is that all? You don't need permission for anything here. Make yourself at home. Help yourself to anything you want."

Still the boy stood, and he tapped the floor impatiently.

Hendon was confused. "Goodness, what is it?"

"Please pour the water, and don't talk so much."

Suppressing a laugh, Hendon thought, "By all the saints, how amazing!" He went over quickly and did the insolent boy's bidding. Then he stood there, astonished, until the command "The towel!" woke him sharply. He took a towel from under the boy's nose and handed it to him without comment. He then washed his own face. Meanwhile the adopted child sat down at the table and prepared to eat. Hendon drew back the other chair and was about to sit when the boy said indignantly, "Wait! You sit in the presence of the king?"

This blow shook Hendon to his foundations. He thought, "The poor thing's madness has changed with the great change in the realm. Now he thinks that he's the king. I must humor him. Otherwise he'll order me to the Tower." Pleased with this joke, he removed the chair from the table, stood behind the king, and proceeded to wait on him in the courtliest way he could.

When the king ate, his royal dignity relaxed a little and he wanted to talk. He asked, "Did I hear you say that you are Miles Hendon?"

"Yes, sire," Hendon replied, then observed to himself, "To humor the poor lad, I must 'sire' him and 'majesty' him. I must play along for his own good."

The king warmed his heart with a second glass of wine and said, "I want to know all about you. Tell me your story. You seem gallant and noble. Are you from a noble family?"

"We are modest members of the nobility, your majesty. My father is a baronet, one of the smaller lords, through his service as a knight: Sir Richard Hendon of Hendon Hall, by Monk's Holm in Kent."

"The name is not familiar. Go on. Tell me your story."

"It's not much, your majesty, but it will entertain you for half an hour. My father is rich and generous. My mother died when I was a boy. I have two brothers: Arthur, the eldest, with a soul like our father's, and Hugh, the youngest—greedy, treacherous, and vicious. He has been like that his whole life. The last time I saw him was ten years ago, when he was nineteen. I was twenty then, and Arthur twenty-two. The only other relative is Lady Edith, my cousin. She was sixteen when I left. She is beautiful, gentle, and good—an earl's daughter, the last member of her family, and heiress of a great fortune. My father was her guardian. I loved her, and she loved me. But she was engaged to Arthur from the cradle, and my father would not allow the contract to be broken. Arthur loved another maid and told us that somehow Edith and I would be together. Hugh loved Lady Edith's fortune, although he said that he loved *her*. She didn't believe him. No one did, except my father. He loved Hugh best of us all, partly because Hugh is the youngest child. My father also trusted Hugh, who has a persuasive tongue and a gift for lying.

"I was wild, probably very wild, although it hurt only me. I brought shame to no one and never did anything dishonorable. My brother Hugh took advantage of my faults. Because my brother Arthur was not in good health, Hugh thought that he could profit by getting me out of the way. It is a long story, your highness, and hardly worth telling. My brother turned my faults into crimes. By planting a ladder in my room and creating other false evidence, he convinced my father that I planned to defy him and elope with Edith. My father said that three years of banishment from home and England might make a soldier and a man of me and teach me some wisdom. I fought in the continental wars, enduring hardship. In my last battle I was taken captive and held prisoner for seven years. Finally I escaped and fled to London. I have only just arrived, with almost nothing, and no idea of what has happened to my family. That is my meager tale."

"You have been treated shamefully," the little king said with flashing eyes. "I swear I will put it right. The king declares it." Fired by the story of Hendon's wrongs, he spilled the history of his own recent misfortune into the ears of his astonished listener.

When he had finished, Hendon thought, "My, what an imagination he has! Truly this is no common mind, or else it could not weave such a straight and dramatic tale out of the air. Poor little boy. He will not be homeless or lonely while I am alive. He will never leave my side and will be my little comrade. And he will be cured. Then he will make something of himself. How proud I will be to say, 'Yes, he is mine. I took him in, a homeless little ragamuffin, but I saw what was in him. I said that he would amount to something. Now look at him. Wasn't I right?'"

The king spoke thoughtfully. "You saved me from injury and shame and possibly death. Therefore, you protected my crown. Such service deserves rich reward. Name your wish. If it is within my power, I will grant it."

This fantastic suggestion startled Hendon out of his thoughts. He was about to thank the king and say that he had only done his duty and desired no reward, but a wiser idea came to him. He asked permission to consider the gracious offer for a few moments—an idea that the king gravely approved, remarking that it was best to be careful with such an important decision. Hendon reflected, then said to himself, "Yes, that is the thing to do. It would be impossible to achieve any other way, and I cannot go on like this. I will propose it. It is good that I didn't waste this chance."

He dropped to one knee and said, "My poor service was only a subject's simple duty and therefore deserves no praise. However, because your majesty would like to reward me, I will ask for one thing. Almost four hundred years ago, as your grace knows, there was a feud between John, king of England, and the king of France. It was declared that two champions should fight each other to settle the dispute. These two kings, and the Spanish king, arrived to judge the conflict. The French champion appeared, but he was so fearsome that our English knights refused to fight him. It looked as if the English monarch would lose by default. At this time Lord de Courcy, the mightiest arm in England, lay in the Tower, stripped of his honors and possessions, enduring a long captivity. He was asked to help. He agreed and went forth dressed for battle. As soon as the Frenchman glimpsed his huge frame and heard his famous name, he fled, and the French king lost. King John restored de Courcy's titles and possessions and said, 'Name your wish. You will have it, even if it costs me half my kingdom.' Kneeling as I do now, de Courcy answered, 'Your majesty, I ask that I and my successors may forever have the privilege of leaving our heads covered in the presence of England's kings.' As your majesty knows, the wish was granted. For the last four hundred years, the head of the de Courcy family has worn his hat or helmet in the king's presence, which no one else may do. In light of this story, I beg the king to grant me one privilege: that I and my heirs, forever, may sit in the presence of England's majesty."

"Rise, Sir Miles Hendon, knight," the king said gravely, touching Hendon's shoulders with his sword. "Rise and be seated. Your request is granted. While England remains and the crown continues, your privilege will continue."

The king paced the floor, thinking. Hendon dropped into a chair at the table, observing to himself, "That was a good idea. My legs are weary. If I had not thought of that, I might have had to stand for weeks, until my poor boy recovered his wits. And so, I am a knight of the Kingdom of

Dreams and Shadows. A strange position for someone as practical as I am. I will not laugh, God forbid, because what is imaginary to me is real to him. In a way, though, it is real to me because it shows the boy's sweet and generous nature." Then he had this thought: "Ah, what if he were to call me by my fine title in public? There would be an amusing contrast between my glory and my clothing. No matter. Let him call me what he will. If it pleases him, I am happy."

CHAPTER 13

The King's Disappearance

Soon the two friends became very sleepy. The king said, "Remove these rags," meaning his clothing.

Hendon undressed the boy and tucked him into bed. Then he glanced around the room, thinking, "He has taken my bed again. What will I do?"

The little king saw his confusion and offered a solution by saying sleepily, "You will sleep in front of the door and guard it." In a moment the king was resting in a deep slumber.

"Dear heart, he should have been born a king," Hendon muttered admiringly. "He plays the part perfectly." He lay down on the floor in front of the door, thinking, "I have lived worse for seven years. It would be ungrateful to God to complain about this." He dropped into sleep as the dawn appeared.

Toward noon Hendon rose, uncovered his sleeping ward, and measured the boy's body with a string. The king awoke just as he had completed his work. The boy complained of the cold and asked what he was doing.

"It's done, your highness," Hendon said. "I

have a bit of business outside, but I will return soon. You should go back to sleep. Let me cover your head also, to make you warmer."

The king was back in dreamland before this speech ended. Hendon slipped softly out and slipped as softly in again thirty or forty minutes later with a complete secondhand suit of boy's clothing. It was of cheap material and showed signs of wear, but it was tidy and right for the season. He seated himself and began to look over his purchase, mumbling to himself. "More money would have gotten a better one, but when one is short on funds, one must be happy with less."

Hendon began to sing: "There was a woman in our town, in our town did dwell." Then he thought, "He stirred. I must sing more quietly. He needs his rest for the journey. This piece of clothing is not too bad. A stitch here and another one there will fix it. This other one is better, but it also could use some fixing. These shoes are very good and sound and will keep his small feet warm and dry. Probably this will be an odd, new thing to him because he has been barefoot through many winters and summers. If only needles were free and thread were as cheap as bread. I will have a devil of a time threading this one." And so he had. He did as men always have done and probably always will do: he held the needle still and tried to thrust the thread through the eye, which is the opposite of a woman's way. Time and time again the thread missed the mark, going sometimes on one side of the needle, sometimes on the other, and sometimes doubling up against the shaft. But he was patient, having been through frustrating things when he was soldiering. He finally succeeded and began working on the garment in his lap.

"The inn is paid, including the next breakfast," Hendon told himself. "There is enough left to buy a couple of donkeys and pay our traveling costs between here and the riches that await us at Hendon Hall." He resumed his singing: "She loved her hus..."

Hendon drove the needle under his nail. "Ow!" The wound was slight, so he returned to thinking about the future. "We will be happy at Hendon Hall, little one. Never doubt it. Your troubles will vanish there, and you'll regain your health."

Hendon sang again: "She loved her husband dearly, but another man..." His thoughts interrupted as he held up the garment and admired it. "These large stitches look noble. They have a grandeur and majesty that make the tailor's small, stingy ones look ordinary." He sang some more— "She loved her husband dearly, but another man he loved her"—and viewed his handiwork. "It's done, and it's a nice job," he thought. "Now I will wake him, dress him, pour for him, and feed him. Then we will go to the market by the Tabard Inn in Southwark."

Hendon said, "Please rise, my liege." No answer. "Your majesty." Hendon threw back the covers. "What?" The boy was gone! Hendon looked around in speechless astonishment and noticed that his ward's ragged clothing also was missing. He began to rage and storm and shout for the innkeeper.

At that moment a servant entered with the breakfast. "Explain, servant of Satan, or your time is at an end!" Hendon roared, He sprang at the waiter so savagely that the man was speechless from surprise and fright. "Where is the boy?"

The man spoke in a trembling voice. "You had just left, your worship, when a youth came running and said that you wanted the boy to meet you at the Bridge's Southwark end. I brought him up to the room. When he woke the lad and gave his message, the lad grumbled about being disturbed 'so early,' as he called it. But he immediately dressed and went with the youth, saying that it would have been more polite to come yourself, so..."

"So you are a fool and easily deceived. But maybe it will turn out all right. I will go fetch him. Make the table ready. Wait! The bedclothes were arranged as if someone were in them. Did that happen by accident?"

"I don't know, your worship. I saw the youth meddle with them, the one who came for the boy."

"A thousand deaths! It was done to deceive me and gain time. Listen. Was that youth alone?"

"All alone, your worship."

"Are you sure?"

"Sure, your worship."

"Collect your scattered wits. Think carefully, man."

After a moment's thought the servant said, "When he came, no one came with him. But now I remember that as the two stepped into the crowd on the Bridge, a rough man plunged out from nearby. Just as he was joining them..."

"What then? Out with it!" Hendon thundered.

"Just then the crowd swallowed them up. I saw no more, being called by my master, who was angry because a hinge had not been delivered. Blaming me for that hinge is like blaming an unborn child for sins com..."

"Out of my sight, idiot! Your chatter drives me mad. Hold on! Did they go toward Southwark?"

"Yes, your worship. As I said before about that stupid hinge, an unborn child is no more blameless than..."

"You're still here complaining? Vanish, or I'll strangle you."

The servant vanished.

Hendon followed after him, passed him, and plunged down the stairs two at a time. "It's that awful villain who claimed that he was his son," Hendon thought. "I have lost you, my poor little mad master. It is a bitter thought because I have come to love you. No, you are not lost; I will search until I find you. Poor child, our breakfast is waiting. I have no hunger now. Let the rats eat it.

I must hurry." As he rushed through the crowd on the Bridge, he thought with satisfaction, "He grumbled, but he went—sweet lad—because he thought that *I* had asked it. He would not have done it for anyone else."

CHAPTER 14

Royal Routine

That morning Tom Canty awoke from a heavy sleep and opened his eyes in the dark. He lay silent a few moments, trying to make sense of his thoughts. Then he burst out happily, "Thank God, I am awake! Nan! Bet! Kick off your straw and come here, so that I can tell you the wildest dream that anyone ever had. Nan! Bet!"

A dim form appeared at his side. "What would you command?"

"Command? Oh, woe is me, I know your voice. Tell me. Who am I?"

"You? Yesterday you were the Prince of Wales. Today you are my most gracious liege, Edward, king of England."

Tom buried his head in his pillows, murmuring, "Alas, it was no dream. Sweet sir, please leave me to my sorrows."

Tom slept again and had this pleasant dream. It was summer, and he was playing alone in a pretty meadow. A dwarf only a foot high, with long red whiskers and a humped back, suddenly appeared and said, "Dig by that stump." Tom did so and found twelve bright new pennies.

Wonderful riches! But this was only the beginning. The dwarf said, "I know you. You are a good, deserving lad. Your troubles will end. Today you will be rewarded. Dig here every seventh day, and you always will find the same treasure: twelve bright new pennies. Tell no one this secret." The dwarf vanished, and Tom hurried to Offal Court with his prize, thinking, "Every night I will give my father a penny. He will be happy, thinking that I begged for it, and he will stop beating me. I'll give one penny every week to the good priest who teaches me. The rest will go to Mother, Nan, and Bet. No more hunger and rags; no more fears and abuse." In his dream he reached his home all out of breath, but his eyes danced with enthusiasm. He threw four pennies into his mother's lap and cried, "They are for you, Nan, and Bet! All of them. They are honestly come by, not begged or stolen." His happy, astonished mother hugged him and exclaimed, "It's getting late. Would your majesty like to rise?"

Ah, that was not the answer he was expecting. The dream had come apart, and he was awake. He opened his eyes to see the richly dressed First Lord of the Bedchamber kneeling by his couch. The happiness of his dream faded away as the poor boy realized that he still was a captive and a king. The room was filled with courtiers clothed in cloaks of purple, the mourning color, and with royal servants. Tom sat up in bed and, from behind the heavy silk curtains, gazed out at this group.

The serious business of dressing began. As it proceeded, one courtier after another knelt and offered the little king sympathies for his heavy loss. A shirt was picked up by the Chief Supervisor of the Royal Horses, who passed it to the First Lord of the Buckhounds, who passed it to the Second Gentleman of the Bedchamber, who passed it to the Head Ranger of Windsor Forest, who passed it to the Third Groom of the Stole, who passed it to the Royal Chancellor of the Duchy of Lancaster, who passed it to the Master of the Wardrobe, who passed it to the Master of Arms, who passed it to the Constable of the Tower, who passed it to the Chief Steward of the Household, who passed it to the Hereditary Grand Diaperer, who passed it to the Lord High Admiral, who passed it to the Archbishop of Canterbury, who passed it to the First Lord of the Bedchamber, who took what was

left of it and put it on Tom. The process reminded the poor little chap of passing buckets at a fire.

Each garment had to go through this slow
process. Consequently, Tom grew so weary of the
ceremony that he felt grateful when he finally saw
his long silk hose begin the journey down the line.
This meant that the end of the matter was drawing
near. But he had celebrated too soon. The First
Lord of the Bedchamber received the hose and
was about to put them on Tom's legs when he
blushed. With an astounded look, he hustled the
things back into the Archbishop of Canterbury's
hands. Whispering, "See, my lord!" he pointed to
something connected with the hose. The
Archbishop paled, then flushed, and passed the
hose to the Lord High Admiral, whispering, "See,
my lord!" The Admiral passed the hose to the
Hereditary Grand Diaperer and hardly had breath
enough in his body to exclaim, "See, my lord!"
The hose drifted backward along the line to the
Chief Steward of the Household, Constable of the
Tower, Master of Arms, Master of the Wardrobe,
Royal Chancellor of the Duchy of Lancaster, Third
Groom of the Stole, Head Ranger of Windsor
Forest, Second Gentleman of the Bedchamber,
and First Lord of the Buckhounds until they final-
ly reached the hands of the Chief Supervisor of the
Royal Horses, who looked with a pale face at what
had caused all this dismay. He hoarsely whispered,
"Heavens, a missing lace! To the Tower with the
Head Keeper of the King's Hose!" Then he leaned

on the shoulder of the First Lord of the Buckhounds to regain his strength while fresh hose, without any damaged strings, were brought.

But all things must end, and Tom finally was able to get out of bed. The proper official poured water, the proper official did the washing, the proper official stood by with a towel, and Tom got safely through the cleansing stage and was ready for the Royal Hairdresser's services. When Tom eventually emerged in purple satin pants, jacket, and cloak and a plumed purple cap, he was as elegant and pretty as a girl. He went to his breakfast room through a crowd of assembled courtiers. As he passed, everyone made way for him and dropped to their knees.

After breakfast his highest-ranking officers and fifty guards holding gold battle-axes accompanied him, with regal ceremony, to the throne room, where he proceeded to conduct national business. Lord Hertford stood by the throne to assist him with advice.

A group of men appointed by Henry the Eighth asked Tom to approve certain acts of theirs. The Archbishop of Canterbury reported on the arrangements for Henry the Eighth's funeral and read the signatures of the executors: the Archbishop of Canterbury, Lord Chancellor of England, William Lord St. John, John Lord Russell, Edward Earl of Hertford, John Viscount Lisle, Cuthbert Bishop of Durham...

Tom was not listening because an earlier part

of the document was puzzling him. He turned and whispered to Lord Hertford, "What day did he say the burial is scheduled for?"

"The sixteenth of next month, your majesty."

"That is strange. Will his body keep?" Poor chap, he still was new to royal customs. He was used to seeing Offal Court's abandoned dead hustled out of the way. Lord Hertford reassured him.

A secretary of state asked the king to approve the reception of foreign ambassadors for eleven o'clock the next day. Tom looked at Hertford, who whispered, "Your majesty should agree. They come to offer their kings' sympathies." Tom did as he was advised.

Another secretary began to read a report of the late king's household expenses, which amounted to £28,000 over the last six months. This amount was so large that it made Tom gasp. He gasped again when he found out that £20,000 of this amount still was unpaid, that the king's money was almost gone, and that his twelve hundred servants had not received their salaries. Tom spoke, showing his shock. "It's obvious that we are headed for the poorhouse. We need to move to a smaller home and let the servants go. They only slow us down and make us dependent on them. I remember a small house over by the fish market..." A sharp pressure on Tom's arm silenced him and made him blush. But nobody appeared to notice his strange comments.

A secretary reported that the late king's will

had made the Earl of Hertford into a duke; Hertford's brother, Sir Thomas Seymour, into an earl; and Hertford's son into an earl. The council had decided to make these and other honors official on February 16th. Because the late king had not declared how much land these men should receive, the council had decided to give Seymour land worth £500 and Hertford land worth £1,100, provided that the new king gave his permission. Tom was going to blurt out that the late king's debts should be paid before any more money was squandered, but the watchful Hertford touched Tom's arm, preventing any such outburst. Feeling uncomfortable, Tom gave the royal assent without commenting.

But then he had a happy thought: Why not make his mother Duchess of Offal Court and give her an estate? No, he was a king only in name. These serious men were his masters, and they would think his mother the invention of a crazed mind. They would listen to his idea with unbelieving ears and send for the doctor.

The dull work went on. Petitions, proclamations, patents, and all sorts of wordy, repetitious, and boring papers relating to public business were read. Tom sighed and thought, "What have I done wrong that God saw fit to shut me up here—away from freedom, fields, and sunshine—and make me a king?" His poor confused head dropped to his shoulder in sleep, and the empire's business came to a halt. The officials of the realm fell silent.

Later that morning Hertford and St. John allowed Tom an enjoyable hour with Lady Elizabeth and little Lady Jane Grey. But the princesses were sad about the king's death. Also, at the end of the visit, his "elder sister" (history's "Bloody Mary") scared him with a serious conversation. The only thing he liked about her was that she didn't stay long.

Tom had a few moments to himself, and then a slim lad about twelve years old was admitted. The lad's clothing was all black except for a white collar and white lace around his wrists. As a sign of mourning he wore a knot of purple ribbon on his shoulder. He walked hesitantly, bowing his head, and dropped onto one knee in front of Tom, who observed him seriously for a moment and then said, "Rise, lad. Who are you? What do you want?"

The boy rose and looked concerned. "Surely you remember me, my lord. I am your whipping boy."

"My whipping boy?"

"Yes, your grace. I am Humphrey Marlow."

Tom thought that his advisors should have told him about the boy. The situation was delicate. What should he do? If he pretended to know the lad, everything he said would reveal otherwise. What if this sort of thing continued to happen? He needed a strategy to deal with such situations. He decided to try one out. After rubbing his forehead a moment or two, he said, "Now I somewhat remember you, but my mind is confused with grief."

"My poor master!" the whipping boy exclaimed, adding to himself, "It is just as they said. His mind is gone. Alas, poor soul. But look how I forget. They said that I must not appear to notice that something is wrong."

"It's strange how my memory plays tricks on me these days," Tom said. "Pay no attention. I will get better quickly. A little clue usually is enough to remind me. Tell me your business."

"It is a small thing, your majesty, but I will tell you. Two days ago, when your majesty made three mistakes in your Greek lessons . . . Do you remember?"

"Ye...es, I think I do," Tom replied, thinking, "It is not much of a lie. I must have made forty mistakes." He continued, "Yes, I recall it now. Go on."

"The master, angry at what he called inferior work, promised that he would soundly whip me for it and..."

"Whip *you*?" Tom asked, too astonished to hold back. "Why would he whip *you* for *my* mistakes?"

"Ah, your grace forgets again. He always punishes me when you fail in your lessons."

"True. I had forgotten. You mean that you teach me in private. If I fail, he believes that you didn't do your job well and..."

"Oh, your grace, what are you talking about? I, your humblest servant, never would attempt to teach you!"

"Then, how are you at fault? Have I truly

gone mad, or have *you*? Explain it to me."

"Your majesty, there's nothing to explain. No one may harm the sacred body of a prince or king. Therefore, when you fail, I am punished. This is my duty and profession."

Tom stared at the calm boy, thinking, "What a strange job! I am amazed that they have not hired a boy to be combed and dressed for me. I wish that they would. If they did, I would take my own lashings and be thankful for the change." He said aloud, "And have you received the beating, poor friend?"

"No, your majesty. My punishment was scheduled for today, and it might be canceled because this is a time of mourning. I am not sure, so I have boldly come here to remind your grace about your generous promise to argue for me."

"With the master? To prevent your whipping?"

"Ah, you remember."

"Yes. My memory improves. Do not worry. Your back will not be hurt. I will see to it."

"Thank you, my good lord!" the boy cried, dropping to one knee again. "Perhaps I have gone far enough, but..."

Tom encouraged Humphrey to continue, saying that he was "in the granting mood."

"Then, I will tell you because it is important to me. Now that you are king, you can do whatever you choose. You probably will want to replace your studies with less boring activities. But if you do, I will be ruined, along with my orphan sisters."

"Ruined? How?"

"My back is my bread, your grace. If it does not suffer, I starve. If you quit your studies, my job will be gone because you won't need a whipping boy. Please do not turn me away!"

Tom was touched by this pathetic distress. With a royal burst of generosity, he said, "Worry no more, lad. Your job will belong to you and your heirs forever." He lightly touched the boy's shoulder with the flat of his sword, exclaiming, "Rise, Humphrey Marlow, Hereditary Grand Whipping Boy to England's royal house. Take heart. I will return to my books and study so poorly that they will have to triple your salary because of the extra work you will perform."

The grateful Humphrey exclaimed, "Thank you, noble master. This great gift goes far beyond my wildest dreams. Now I will be happy forever, and so will my heirs."

Tom was smart enough to realize that the boy could be useful to him. He encouraged Humphrey to talk, which the lad was happy to do. Humphrey was delighted to believe that he was helping in Tom's "cure." Whenever he told Tom details of the prince's royal life in the schoolroom and elsewhere in the palace, Tom then was able to "remember" them clearly. At the end of an hour, Tom had gained valuable information about court matters and people. In order to continue this education, he decided that Humphrey would be admitted to the royal apartment whenever he came, provided that other people were not present.

Humphrey had just left when Lord Hertford arrived with more trouble for Tom. He said that the lords of the council, afraid that the rumor of the king's damaged health might have leaked out, had decided that his majesty should begin to dine in public after a day or two. His wholesome and energetic appearance, together with his graceful behavior, would squash the rumors.

Under the thin disguise of "reminding" Tom of things that he already knew, the earl proceeded to gently instruct Tom about the proper way to behave on such occasions,. To the earl's relief, Tom needed little help after talking to Humphrey, who had told Tom that he soon would be dining in public and had answered Tom's questions on that subject.

Seeing the royal memory so improved, the earl decided to test it in an apparently casual way. The results were good in the areas covered by Humphrey, and the earl was encouraged enough to say, "Now, I believe that if you try a little harder, you can solve the puzzle of the Great Seal. Its loss is no longer important because its value ended with the late king's life, but perhaps your grace can solve the puzzle. Do you feel up to trying?"

Tom had no idea what the Great Seal was. After hesitating, he looked up innocently and asked, "What was it like, my lord?"

The earl was taken aback. "Alas, his wits are

gone again," he thought. "It was a bad idea to demand so much of them." He skillfully changed the subject, and Tom forgot all about the Seal.

CHAPTER 15

English Law

The next day, the foreign ambassadors came, with their beautiful attendants. Tom received them from his majestic throne. At first he was delighted by all the splendor, but the audience was gloomy, and so were most of the speeches. His pleasure eventually changed to boredom and homesickness. Tom said whatever Hertford told him to and tried hard to behave well, but he was too uncomfortable to do a very good job. He looked like a king, but he didn't feel like one. He was glad when the ceremony ended. Most of his day was "wasted" (as he called it) in royal duties. Even the two hours of recreation were not very entertaining, with all their restrictions and ceremonies. However, he had a private hour with his whipping boy that he thought was worthwhile because he got both entertainment and important information out of it.

The third day of Tom's kingship came and went much as the others had, but it was slightly better in one way: he was getting a little more used to his surroundings. His imprisonment still bothered him but not all the time. He found that being around nobles bothered him less with every passing hour.

If he hadn't been required to dine in public, he would have been at ease on the fourth day. His schedule for the day included activities more important than public dining, such as forming his foreign policy and promoting Hertford to the position of Lord Protector, but nothing intimidated Tom like the idea of eating in front of a crowd, all talking about his manners and mistakes. So the fourth day found Tom gloomy and forgetful, and he could not shake off this mood. As the morning dragged on, filled with his boring duties as king, he felt more like a prisoner than ever. Late in the morning he was talking with the Earl of Hertford while waiting for a visit from a group of officials. After a little while, Tom wandered to a window and watched the people moving outside the palace gates. He longed to be back among them. Then he saw a group of poor men, women, and children shouting and traveling down the road. "I wish I knew what that is about!" he exclaimed, with a boy's curiosity.

"You are the king," the earl solemnly responded. "Will you allow me to find out?"

"Gladly!" Tom exclaimed, adding to himself, "In truth, being a king is not all dreariness; it has its rewards."

The earl called a page and sent him to the captain of the guard with the order, "Stop the mob, and ask what it is doing, by the king's command."

A few seconds later a row of royal guards, dressed in flashing steel, filed out at the gates and blocked the highway in front of the crowd. A messenger returned and reported that the mob was following a man, woman, and young girl to execution for crimes committed against the realm's dignity.

A violent death for these poor unfortunates! The idea pulled Tom's heartstrings. He was seized by compassion, with no thought for the broken laws or injured victims. He could think only about the hanging platform and the gory fate awaiting the condemned. His concern even made him forget, for the moment, that he was a false king. Before he knew it, he had blurted out the command, "Bring them here." Then he blushed and was on the verge of apologizing. But after seeing that his order had not surprised anyone, he said nothing. The page, in the most matter-of-fact way, bowed low and walked backward out of the room to deliver the command. Feeling proud of his decision, Tom thought again about the advantages of being the king. He said to himself, "It is like the times that I read the old priest's tales and imagined myself a prince who could command anything of anyone."

Now the doors swung open. One important title after another was announced, followed by the actual people, and the room quickly was half filled with nobles. Being so interested in the other matter, Tom hardly noticed them. He sat in his royal chair and looked impatiently at the audience, who reacted by talking among themselves so as not to disturb him.

In a little while the footsteps of military men

were heard approaching and the criminals entered, escorted by an under-sheriff and a few of the king's guards. The under-sheriff knelt before Tom, then stood aside. The three doomed people also knelt, and they remained kneeling. The guards took their position behind Tom's chair.

Curious, Tom inspected the prisoners. Something about the man's dress or appearance seemed familiar. "I think I have seen this man before, but I don't know when or where," Tom thought. Just then the man glanced up and quickly dropped his face again, out of fear and respect. But it was enough to jog Tom's memory. He said to himself, "Now I know. This is the stranger who plucked Giles Witt out of the Thames River and saved his life on that windy, bitter New Year's day. It was a brave, good deed. What a pity he has been doing bad things. I have not forgotten that day and exact hour because an hour later, at the stroke of eleven, Grandma Canty gave me the worst beating of my life."

Tom ordered that the woman and girl be removed from the room. Then he spoke to the under-sheriff. "Good sir, what is this man's offense?"

The officer knelt and answered, "Your majesty, he has killed someone with poison."

Tom's compassion and admiration for the man as a drowning boy's daring rescuer sharply decreased. "Has it been proven?" he asked.

"Most clearly, sire."

Tom sighed and said, "Take him away. He has earned his death. It's a pity because he had a brave heart... I mean he *looks* brave."

The prisoner wrung his hands and begged the "king" in terror, "My lord the king, if you have any pity, then pity me! I am innocent. The crime was not proven. I know that I cannot change the judgment, but I cannot bear my punishment. In your royal compassion, please grant my prayer and command that I be hanged."

Tom was amazed. "What a strange request! Weren't you *going* to be hanged?"

"Oh no, my liege. It is ordered that I be boiled alive."

The hideous surprise of these words almost made Tom leap from his chair. As soon as he recovered his wits, he cried, "Have your wish, poor soul! If you had poisoned a hundred men, you should not have to suffer such a horrible death."

The prisoner bowed his face to the ground and declared, "If, God forbid, you ever know misfortune, may your goodness to me be remembered and rewarded!"

Tom turned to the Earl of Hertford and said, "My lord, is this man's ferocious punishment legal?"

"Your grace, it is the law for poisoners. In Germany poisoners are slowly boiled to death in oil. They are let down into the oil by degrees: first the feet, then the legs, then..."

"No more, my lord. I cannot bear it!" Tom

cried, covering his eyes with his hands to shut out the picture. "I request that this law be changed. Let no more poor creatures be tortured so."

The earl's face showed deep approval because he was a generous and merciful man, which was not common in those days. "Your noble words have sealed the law's doom," he said. "History will remember this honorable act."

The under-sheriff was about to remove his prisoner, but Tom signaled him to wait. "Good sir, I wish to look further into this matter. The man has said that his crime was not proven. Tell me what you know."

"Your grace, the trial revealed that this man entered a house in Islington where someone was sick. Three witnesses say it was ten in the morning; two say it was some minutes later. The sick man was alone, sleeping. After this man left, the sick man died within the hour, being torn with spasms and vomiting."

"Did anyone see the prisoner give the sick man poison? Was poison found?"

"No, my liege."

"Then, how do you know that poison was given at all?"

"Your majesty, the doctors testified that no one dies with such symptoms except by poison."

In that simple age this was heavy evidence. Tom recognized its weight. "The doctor knows his business, so the conclusion probably is right. It doesn't look good for this poor man."

"This was not all, your majesty. There is worse evidence. Many people testified that a witch who used to live in the village predicted that the sick man would be poisoned by a stranger who would have brown hair and wear old, ordinary clothes. This prisoner fits that description perfectly."

This was a convincing argument in that superstitious time. Tom felt that the matter was settled beyond any doubt. Still, he offered the prisoner a chance. "If you have anything to say, then speak."

"Nothing that will help, my king. I am innocent, but I cannot prove it. I have no friends; otherwise, I could prove that I was not in Islington that day. I could show that, at the time in question, I was miles away, at Wapping Old Stairs. I also could show that instead of taking a life, I was saving one. A drowning boy..."

"Peace! Sheriff, name the day that the sick man died."

"New Year's day, most illustrious..."

"Let the prisoner go free. It is the king's will!" Tom blushed after this unroyal outburst. In an attempt to lessen his embarrassment, he added, "It enrages me that a man should be hanged because of such foolish, meaningless evidence."

A buzz of admiration swept through the audience. It was not admiration for Tom's decision; most people did not agree with pardoning a convicted poisoner. No, the admiration was for the intelligence and spirit that Tom had displayed. People commented in low voices.

"This is no mad king. His mind is strong."

"How sanely he put his questions. How like his old self to be so haughty and abrupt."

"God be thanked that his illness has passed! This is no weakling, but a king. He has behaved like his father."

Tom overheard some of the comments, which made him feel satisfied with his decision. However, his childish curiosity overpowered these pleasant thoughts. He was eager to know what crimes the woman and little girl could have committed. So, by his command, the two terrified and sobbing creatures were brought before him.

"What have they done?" he asked the sheriff.

"Your majesty, they have been charged with a wicked crime that has been proven. According to the law, the judges have ordered that they be hanged. They sold themselves to the devil."

Tom shuddered. He had been taught to dislike people who did this evil thing. Still, he was not going to deny his curiosity. "Where was this done, and when?"

"In a ruined church at midnight, in December, your majesty."

Tom shuddered again. "Who was there?"

"Only these two, your grace."

"Have they confessed?"

"No, sire. They deny it."

"Then, how was it known?"

"Witnesses saw them going there, your majesty. This put them under suspicion, and the results of their crime have since confirmed it. In particular, they used their wicked power to bring about a storm that destroyed the area. Over forty people say that they witnessed the storm, and at least a thousand suffered because of it."

"Indeed, this is a serious matter." Tom turned this dark crime over in his mind, then asked, "Did the woman also suffer because of the storm?" Several elders in the audience nodded at this question's wisdom.

The sheriff answered, "She did, your majesty, and very seriously. Her house was swept away, and she and her child were left without shelter."

"If this woman sold her soul, and her child's, and then used her power to cause a storm that harmed them both, she is mad. If she is mad, she doesn't know any better and, therefore, is not guilty."

The elders again nodded. One murmured, "If the king is mad, it is the kind of madness that I wish other people would catch."

"How old is the child?" Tom asked.

"Nine, your majesty."

"Is it legal for a child to sell herself, my lord?" Tom asked, turning to a wise judge.

"No, your majesty. The law does not allow children to enter into contracts because they are too young to understand them."

"In that case, the child, too, wouldn't know what she was doing if she sold herself to the devil." The woman had stopped crying and was hanging on Tom's words with growing hope. Tom noticed this, and it increased his sympathy for her. "How did they cause the storm?" he asked.

"By pulling off their stockings, sire."

"That is amazing!" Tom exclaimed. "Does it always cause a storm?"

"Always, my liege—at least, if the woman wants it and says the right words, either in her mind or out loud."

Tom turned to the woman and eagerly said, "Work your magic. I want to see a storm." The audience paled; they all wanted to run from the room. But Tom paid attention only to the woman. Seeing a puzzled and astonished look on her face, he added excitely, "Never fear; you will not be blamed. To the contrary, you will go free. Go ahead; show your power."

"Oh, my lord, I don't have any power. I have been falsely accused."

"You are afraid. Do not worry. No one will harm you. Make a storm. It doesn't matter how small it is. I don't need anything big or dangerous. In fact, I prefer the opposite. Do this, and I'll spare your life. You will leave free, with your child, holding the king's pardon."

The woman threw herself onto the floor and tearfully protested that she had no power to do the miracle; otherwise, she certainly would create a storm in order to save her child's life.

"I think the woman is honest," Tom said. "If my mother were in her place and had the devil's powers, she would not hesitate to cause a storm in order to save my life. All mothers are the same. You are free, good wife—you and your child—because I think you are innocent. You are pardoned."

The woman passionately expressed her gratitude.

CHAPTER 16

The State Dinner

Although it almost was time for dinner, Tom felt little anxiety. The morning's experiences had given him confidence. After four days the little barn cat already was more comfortable in his strange surroundings than a mature person would have been after a month. It was an example of a child's great ability to adapt.

The banquet room where Tom was to dine was a spacious apartment with gold pillars and painted walls and ceilings. At the door stood tall guards, as rigid as statues, dressed in rich costumes and holding ax-head spears. In a high gallery around the room sat a band of musicians and a crowd of citizens in brilliant clothing. Tom's table was in the center of the room, on a raised platform. A gentleman entered the room, knelt three times, and covered the table with a cloth. After kneeling again, he left. Then another gentleman entered, with a salt shaker, a plate, and bread. He knelt three times, placed the goods on the table, knelt again, and left. Two well-dressed nobles then entered. After kneeling, they solemnly rubbed the table with bread and salt.

Down the hall a bugle blasted, and someone cried, "Make way for the king! Make way for the king's most excellent majesty!" These sounds were repeated, coming nearer and nearer until the shining procession marched through the door. First came gentlemen, barons, earls, and knights of the Garter, all richly dressed. Next came the chancellor, between two guards, one of whom carried the royal scepter, the other the Sword of State in a red sheath studded with gold lilies. Next came the king himself. Twelve trumpets and many drums saluted him with a burst of welcome while everyone in the galleries rose in their places, crying, "God save the King!" After him came his nobles. His guard of honor marched on his right and left, carrying gold battle-axes.

During this fine ceremony Tom's pulse beat quickly, and his eyes twinkled. His mind was charmed by everything that was going on. He carried himself gracefully, all the more so because he was not thinking about how he was doing it. Besides, no one can be very ungraceful in beautiful, nicely fitting clothes after he has grown a little used to them. Tom remembered his instructions and acknowledged his greeting with a slight nod of his plumed head and a courteous "I thank you, my good people." He sat down at the table, and the procession broke up into groups.

The Yeomen of the Guard, England's tallest and mightiest men, entered to lively music. They were clothed in scarlet, with gold roses on their backs. They went in and out of the room, bringing a course of dishes served on plates. Another gentleman took the dishes and placed them on the table while the taster gave each guard a mouthful of the particular dish that he had brought, to test for poison.

Tom ate well, in spite of feeling hundreds of eyes on him. He was careful not to hurry and equally careful not to do anything for himself; instead, he waited until the proper official knelt down and did it for him. He got through without a mistake.

When the meal finally ended, he marched away in the procession, accompanied by blaring bugles, rolling drums, and thunderous applause. If that was the worst of dining in public, he would be glad to endure it several times a day, provided it would free him from some of his other responsibilities.

CHAPTER 17

Foo-Foo the First

Miles Hendon hurried toward London Bridge's Southwark end, keeping a sharp lookout and hoping to catch up with the king and his captors. He was disappointed, however. By asking questions, he was able to track them part of the way through Southwark. Then all traces ceased, and he didn't know where to go. Still, he continued looking for the rest of the day. By nightfall he was exhausted and hungry and had made no headway. So he dined at the Tabard Inn and went to bed, resolved to make an early start in the morning and search the entire town.

As he lay in bed, Hendon thought, "If possible, the boy will escape from the ruffian, his supposed father. Will he return to London and his old neighborhood? No, that would mean risking recapture. Having never had any friend other than me, he'll try to find me. He'll head for Hendon Hall because he knows that I'm headed there. I must waste no more time in Southwark. I'll go through Kent toward Monk's Holm, searching the woods and inquiring as I go."

Let us now return to the vanished king. The

ruffian, whom the waiter at the inn saw "joining" the king and the youth who had come for him, didn't actually join them. Instead, saying nothing, he followed them. His left arm was in a sling, and he wore a green patch over one eye. He limped slightly, using a wooden stick as a support.

The youth led the king crookedly through Southwark and occasionally went onto the main road. The king became irritated and said that he was stopping: it was Hendon's duty to come to him, not his to go to Hendon; he would not endure such disrespect.

The youth said, "You want to stop here when your friend lies wounded in the woods?"

The king's attitude immediately changed. "Wounded?" he cried. "Who has dared to do it? But that doesn't matter. Lead on, lead on. Faster, fool! Are your shoes made of lead? Wounded, is he? The person responsible will be sorry even if he is a duke's son."

It was some distance to the woods, but they went quickly. The youth looked around and discovered a branch stuck in the ground, with a bit of rag tied to it. Then he led the way into the forest, looking for similar branches and finding them at intervals. Evidently they were guides to his destination.

Eventually they reached a clearing with a farmhouse's burned remains and a decaying barn. It was silent, with no sign of life. The youth entered the barn, with the king eagerly following. No one was there.

The king shot a surprised and suspicious glance at the youth and asked, "Where is he?" A mocking laugh was his answer. The king flew into a rage. He seized a stick and began to run at the youth when he heard another mocking laugh. It was from the lame ruffian, who had been following at a distance. The king turned and said angrily, "Who are you? Why are you here?"

"Put the stick down," the man said. "Be quiet. My disguise is not good enough to prevent you from recognizing your father."

"You are not my father. I don't know you. I am the king. If you have hidden my servant, find him for me, or you will be sorry for what you've done."

John Canty replied in a stern voice, "You have gone mad. I don't want to punish you, but I will if you provoke me. Your silly talk does no harm here, where no one can hear your foolishness. But you must practice talking normally, so that you won't cause trouble when we leave here. I have murdered someone, so I can't stay at home. Neither can you because you must help me. To be safe, I have changed my name. It is Hobbs, John Hobbs. Yours is Jack. Remember that. Now, speak. Where is your mother? Where are your sisters? They didn't come to the meeting place. Do you know where they went?"

The king answered sullenly, "Don't annoy me with these riddles. My mother is dead, and my sisters are in the palace."

The youth gave a sarcastic laugh. The king would have assaulted him except that Canty prevented him and said, "Peace, Hugo, do not upset him. His mind is sick, and your behavior bothers him. Sit down, Jack, and be quiet. You will have a morsel to eat soon."

Canty and Hugo talked together in low voices, and the king went as far as he could from their disagreeable company. He withdrew to the end of the barn, where a foot of straw covered the dirt floor. He lay down there, pulled straw over himself, and was lost in his thoughts. He had many sad ones, but the saddest was the loss of his father. To the rest of the world the name of Henry the Eighth brought a shiver. It made them think of a monster whose nostrils breathed destruction and whose hands dealt out torture and death. But to this boy the name called up a gentle and affectionate face. He cried openly, remembering loving conversations. As the afternoon passed, the lad, exhausted by grief, fell into a calm sleep.

After a while, he awoke, wondering where he was and what had been happening. He could hear rain falling softly on the roof. A comforting feeling came over him, but it was ruined by a chorus of laughter. Startled, he uncovered his head to see where it came from. An ugly picture met his eye. A bright fire was burning in the middle of the floor at the barn's other end. Around it, weirdly lit by the glare, lay a diverse company of ragged bums and ruffians. There were huge, beefy men, tanned, long-haired, and dressed in outlandish rags; middle-sized youths with angry faces; blind beggars with patched or bandaged eyes; crippled ones with wooden legs and crutches. There was a wicked-looking peddler with his pack; a knife-grinder, a tinker, and a barber with the tools of their trades. There were teenage girls and grown women, including old and wrinkled hags. All of the girls and women were loud, foul-mouthed, and dirty. There were three sickly babies. There were a couple of starving dogs, with strings around their necks, whose job was to lead the blind.

It was night, and the gang had just finished feasting. A can of liquor was passing from mouth to mouth. A general cry broke out: "A song! A song from the Blind Mouse and the Cripple!" One of the blind men got up. He removed the patches that covered his seeing eyes and cast aside the pitiful sign that recited the cause of his misery. The Cripple took off his wooden leg and stood on healthy legs beside his fellow con artist. Then they roared a rowdy tune. At the end of each verse the whole crew joined them in a rousing chorus. After the last verse, the group's half-drunken enthusiasm was so great that everyone sang the song clear through from the beginning, making the rafters shake.

Conversation followed. It revealed that Canty had trained in the gang years ago. The gang asked what he had been doing since then. When he said that he had "accidentally" killed a man, they expressed satisfaction. When he added that the man was a priest, he was roundly applauded and had to take a drink with everyone. Old acquaintances welcomed him joyously, and new ones were proud to shake his hand. He was asked why he had stayed away so many months.

"London is better than the country because the laws aren't as strictly enforced there. If it weren't for that accident, I would have stayed there." He asked how many people the gang had now.

The "Ruffler," or chief, answered, "Twenty-five sturdy members. Most are here; the rest are wandering eastward along the winter route. We'll follow them at dawn."

"I don't see Wen here. Where is he?"

"Poor lad, he eats hot brimstone now. He was killed in a fight this summer."

"I am sad to hear that. Wen was a capable and brave man."

"Indeed, he was. Black Bess, his lover, is still with us, but she has gone eastward. She is a fine lass, well behaved and never drunk more than four days of the week."

"I remember that she always was strict and good. Her mother was a troublesome, short-tempered woman but smarter than most."

"We lost her, though. Her palm reading and other fortune-telling gave her a witch's reputation. The law roasted her to death at a slow fire. It was touching to see the gallant way she met her fate, cursing and abusing the crowd, which gawked at her, while the flames approached her face and burned her thin gray locks. You could live a thousand years and never hear such skilled cursing. Alas, her talent died with her. There are poor imitations left, but no disrespect like hers."

The Ruffler sighed, and the listeners sighed in sympathy. For a moment a general depression fell on the company because even hardened criminals feel emotion once in a while. However, a deep drink all around soon cheered everyone.

"Have any of our other friends fared badly?" Canty asked.

"Some, particularly newcomers, such as small farmers whose farms were taken from them to be changed to sheep ranges. They begged and were whipped in public until their blood ran. Then they were set in the stocks to be pelted. They begged again, were whipped again, and were deprived of an ear. When they begged a third time—poor devils, what else could they do?—they were branded on the cheek with a red-hot iron and sold into slavery. They ran away, were hunted down, and were hanged. Others of us have done better. Stand forth, Yokel, Burns, and Hodge. Show your decorations."

These men stood up and took off some of their rags, exposing their backs, crisscrossed with ropy old welts left by the whip. One lifted his hair and showed the place where a left ear once had been. Another showed a brand on his shoulder—the letter V—and a mutilated ear.

The third said, "I am Yokel, once a prosperous farmer with a loving wife and kids. Now I have a different rank, and the wife and kids are gone. Perhaps they are in heaven, maybe in hell. But, thank God, they don't live in England. My good mother earned a living by nursing the sick. When one of them died, the doctors didn't know why, so my mother was burned as a witch while my children watched and wailed. English law. Everyone, lift your cups! Drink to the merciful English law that delivered her from the English hell. Thank you, mates, one and all. My wife and I begged from house to house, bringing the hungry kids with us. But it was a crime to be hungry in England, so they stripped us and whipped us through three towns. Everyone, drink again to merciful English law! Its lash drank deep of my Mary's blood and killed her quickly. She lies in the beggar's graveyard, safe from harm. While the law lashed me from town to town, my children starved. Drink a drop to the poor kids, who never hurt anyone. I begged again, just for a crust, and was pelted and lost an ear. See, here is what's left of it. I begged again, and here is the stump of the other ear that I lost. I begged again and was sold into slavery. If I washed the stain off my cheek, you would see the branded letter S, for 'slave.' Do you understand that word? An English slave stands before you. I have run from my master, and when I am found—may the law be cursed—I will hang."

A voice rang out, "You will not! Today that

law has ended."

All turned and saw the fantastic figure of the little king hurriedly approaching. As he came into the light, the group exploded with questions: "Who is it? Who are you, little man?"

The boy stood confidently in the middle of the surprised group and answered with royal dignity, "I am Edward, king of England." Wild laughter followed, partly mocking and partly delighting in the joke's excellence. The king was stung. "You rude bums, is this how you respond to my royal promise?" He continued speaking angrily, but he was drowned out by laughter and mocking shouts.

Canty made several attempts to make himself heard above the noise and at last succeeded. "Mates, he is my son—a dreamer, a fool, and stark mad. Pay no attention. He thinks he is the king."

"I *am* the king," Edward said turning toward him, "as you soon will be sorry to find out. You have confessed to a murder, and you will hang for it."

"You will betray me? If I get my hands on you..."

"Tsk," the burly Ruffler said, stepping in to save the king and knocking Canty down with his fist. "Have you no respect for kings or Rufflers? If you do that again, I'll hang you myself." Then he said to the king, "You mustn't threaten your friends, lad, or talk badly about them. And you mustn't say that you're the king. That's treason. We are all bad here, but none of us is evil enough to be a traitor. We are loyal to the king. All together now: 'Long live Edward, king of England!'"

"Long live Edward, king of England!" The response from the motley crew came with such thunder that the old building vibrated with the sound.

For an instant the little king's face lit with pleasure. He bowed his head slightly and said seriously, "I thank you, my good people."

This unexpected response threw the company into spasms of laughter. When everyone had calmed down, the Ruffler said firmly but kindly, "Drop it, boy. It is not wise. Amuse yourself, if you must, but choose some title other than 'King of England.'"

A tinker shrieked, "Foo-Foo the First, King of the Mooncalves!"

A roaring shout went up—"Long live Foo-Foo the First, King of the Mooncalves!"—followed by hooting, catcalls, and peals of laughter.

"Bring him here and crown him!"

"Robe him!"

"Scepter him!"

"Enthrone him!"

Before the little king could draw a breath, he was crowned with a tin pail, robed in a tattered blanket, enthroned on a barrel, and given a tinker's soldering iron for a scepter. Then everyone dropped to their knees around him and sent up a chorus of pretend wailings while they wiped their eyes with their ragged sleeves and aprons.

"Be gracious to us, sweet king!"

"Do not step on us pitiful worms, oh noble majesty!"

"Pity your slaves, and comfort them with a royal kick!"

"Warm us with your bright rays, oh flaming sun of kingliness!"

"Bless the ground with your foot, so that we may eat the dirt and become respectable!"

"Please spit on us, sire, so that we can tell our grandchildren of your generous contempt for us and be proud and happy forever!"

But the humorous tinker made the evening's best joke. Kneeling, he pretended to kiss the king's foot and was angrily pushed away. Then he went around begging for a rag to put over the place on his face that had been touched by the foot, saying it must be preserved from contact with the ordinary air. He planned to make his fortune by going on the road and showing it to people at the rate of a hundred shillings. He was so funny that he won the admiration of the whole shabby group.

Tears of shame and anger came to the little monarch's eyes, and he thought, "They act as though I have wronged them, but my offer was kind. This is how they treat me."

CHAPTER 18

The King with the Vagrants

The troop of vagabonds got up at dawn and started their journey. There was a cloudy sky overhead, wet ground underfoot, and a winter chill in the air. The group no longer was merry. Some were sullen and silent, some were irritable and whiny, and all were thirsty.

The Ruffler put the king in Hugo's charge, with some brief instructions, and ordered Canty to stay away from him. He also warned Hugo not to be too rough with the lad.

After a while the weather grew milder, and the clouds lifted a little. The troop stopped shivering, and their spirits began to improve. They grew more and more cheerful and finally began to tease one another and insult passengers along the highway. This showed that they were savoring life again. Everyone they met on the road was plainly afraid of them; no one stood up to them. Occasionally the hooligans snatched laundry from the hedges, in full view of the owners. Instead of protesting, people only seemed grateful that the troop did not take the hedges, too.

By and by, the ruffians invaded a small farmhouse and made themselves at home while the trembling family cleaned out the pantry to furnish them with breakfast. While taking the food, gang members patted the mother and daughters under the chin and made rude jokes, accompanied by coarse laughter. They threw vegetables and bones at the father and sons, making them dodge out of the way, and they applauded loudly when they made a good hit. They ended by buttering the head of one of the daughters, who had objected to some of their behavior. When they left, they threatened to return and burn down the house if any report was made to the authorities.

About noon, after a long and weary walk, the gang stopped behind a hedge on the edge of a large village. They rested for an hour. Then the crew scattered around the village to work their various schemes.

The king was sent with Hugo. They wandered around for a while, Hugo watching for opportunities to do some business but finding none. He finally said, "I see nothing to steal; it is a poor place. So we will beg."

"We? You are suited to it, but I will not beg."

"You will not beg!" Hugo exclaimed, eyeing the king with surprise. "Since when have you reformed?"

"What do you mean?"

"Haven't you begged in London's streets all your life?"

"I? You idiot!"

"Careful with the compliments; you might run out of them soon. Your father says that you have begged your whole life. Maybe he lied. Maybe you even will dare to say that he lied," Hugo scoffed.

"You mean the man you call my father? Yes, he lied."

"Don't go too far with your insanity act. Amuse yourself, but don't get yourself in trouble. If I tell him this, he'll beat you for it."

"Save yourself the bother. I will tell him."

"I like your spirit, but I don't admire your judgment. You'll get enough beatings in this life without inviting them. But let's forget this matter for now. I believe your father. I don't doubt that he can lie, but he has no reason to lie about this. A wise man doesn't lie for nothing. But come, since you don't feel like begging, how should we occupy ourselves? By robbing kitchens?"

"Enough of this foolishness," the king said angrily. "I am tired of it."

Hugo replied angrily, "Now listen, friend. You won't beg, and you won't rob. So be it. But here's what you *will* do. You will play decoy while I beg. Refuse if you dare." The king was about to reply disrespectfully when Hugo interrupted, "Quiet! Here comes someone with a kind face. I'll fall down in a fit. When the stranger runs to me, start wailing and fall onto your knees. Then cry out as if all the devils of misery were in your belly, and say, "Oh sir, it is my poor afflicted brother, and we are friendless. Donate one little penny from your riches to someone on the verge of death!" Be sure to keep wailing. Don't stop until we cheat him of his penny, or else you'll be sorry."

Hugo then began to moan, groan, and roll his eyes, reeling and staggering. When the stranger was near, he fell down in front of him, with a shriek, and began to wriggle and wallow in the dirt in apparent agony.

"Oh dear!" the goodhearted stranger cried. "Poor soul, how he suffers! There, let me help you up."

"Oh, noble sir, wait. God love you for being so generous, but it hurts to be touched when I am like this. My brother there will tell your worship how I am racked with anguish when these fits come over me. A penny, dear sir. A penny to buy a little food. Then leave me to my sorrows."

"A penny? You will have three, you helpless creature." The man fumbled in his pocket and got them out. "There, poor lad. You are welcome to them. Now come here, my boy, and help me carry your ill brother to that house, where..."

"I am not his brother," the king interrupted.

"What? Not his brother?"

"Oh, listen to him," Hugo groaned, then privately ground his teeth. "He denies his own brother, who has one foot in the grave."

"Boy, you are indeed hard of heart if this is your brother. For shame! He is hardly able to move hand or foot. If he is not your brother, who is he?"

"A beggar and a thief. He has gotten your money and also has picked your pocket. If you want to perform a healing miracle, put your stick on his shoulders and trust in God for the rest."

Hugo didn't wait for the miracle. In a moment he was up and off like the wind, the gentleman shouting and following.

The king, thanking heaven for his own release, fled in the opposite direction and did not slow down until he was out of harm's reach. He took the first road he saw and soon put the village behind him. He hurried along for several hours, nervously looking over his shoulder for pursuers.

His fears finally left him, and a grateful sense of security took their place. He realized that he was hungry and very tired. So he stopped at a farmhouse. Before he could speak, he was rudely driven away. His appearance was working against him.

He wandered on, wounded and indignant. He resolved not to be treated badly anymore, but hunger is pride's master. As evening approached, he made an attempt at another farmhouse. Called bad names and threatened with arrest, he promptly moved on.

During the chilly and overcast night, the weary king marched on. He had to keep moving because every time he sat down to rest, the cold soon penetrated him to the bone. The gloomy darkness made the world seem strange. At times he heard voices approach, pass, and fade into silence. He could see nothing of the people except formless, ghostlike blurs, which made him shudder. Occasionally he caught the twinkle of a faraway light or the sound of sheep's bells. Every now and then he heard a dog's lonesome howl. The king felt intensely alone. He stumbled along, occasionally startled by the rustling of dry leaves overhead, which sounded like someone whispering.

Eventually he saw the light of a nearby lantern. He stepped back into the shadows and waited. The lantern stood by a barn's open door. The king waited. There was no sound, and no one stirred. He got so cold, standing still, and the barn looked so welcoming that he finally decided to risk everything and enter. He went quickly and quietly. Just as he was crossing the threshold, he heard voices behind him. He hurriedly hid behind a barrel inside the barn. Two farm laborers came in, bringing the lantern with them. They started working and talking. While they moved around with the light, the king got a good look at a large stall at the barn's far end. He planned to move there when the laborers left. He also saw a pile of horse blankets and decided to use them as well.

By and by, the men finished and went away, taking the lantern and fastening the door behind them. The shivering king made for the blankets as fast as he could in the dark. He gathered them up and safely groped his way to the stall. He made two of the blankets into a bed, then covered himself with the remaining two. He was a glad king now, although the blankets were old and thin and not quite warm enough. They also gave off a strong horsy odor that was almost suffocating. Although the king was hungry and chilly, he also was so tired that he soon fell into a half sleep.

Just as he was about to drop off completely, he felt something touch him. Immediately he was wide awake. The cold horror of that mysterious touch in the dark almost made his heart stand still. He lay motionless and listened, hardly breathing. Nothing stirred. He continued to listen and wait. After what seemed a long time, he began to fall asleep again. All at once he felt the touch again. The boy felt sick with ghostly fears. Should he fly from this mysterious horror? He could not get out of the barn, and the idea of stumbling around in the dark, with some phantom gliding after him and softly touching his cheek or shoulder, was unbearable. But to stay where he was and endure this living death all night... Was that better? No. There was only one way. He must put out his hand and find out what was touching him. Three times he stretched his hand a little way into the dark and snatched it back out of fear. The fourth time, he groped a little farther, and his hand lightly touched something soft and warm. Terrified, he imagined a corpse, newly dead. But before long he groped again. His hand encountered a bunch of long hair. He shuddered but followed up the hair and found what seemed to be a rope. He followed up the rope and found an innocent calf. The "rope" was the calf's tail. The king was ashamed of

having been so frightened by a sleeping calf, but he was delighted to have the calf's company. He was comforted to finally be near a creature with a soft heart and gentle spirit. He stroked the calf's sleek, warm back. The he rearranged his bed nearer to the calf, cuddled up against her back, and drew the covers over them both. In a minute or two he was as warm and comfortable as he ever had been in a plush bed at the royal palace.

Pleasant thoughts came at once, and his life didn't seem so bad. He was sheltered, warm, and free from his criminal captors. The night wind rose, making the old barn quake and sending up moans in the dark. But it was all music to the king now that he was safe and comfortable. Snuggling closer to his calf friend, he drifted into a deep, dreamless sleep. Distant dogs howled, cattle lowed, and sheets of rain fell on the roof. But England's majesty slept undisturbed, and the calf—not embarrassed by sleeping with a king—did the same.

CHAPTER 19

The King with the Peasants

When the king awoke in the early morning, he found that a wet but intelligent rat had made a cozy bed for herself on his chest. Being disturbed now, she scampered away. The boy smiled and thought, "Poor rat, you needn't be afraid. I wouldn't hurt anyone as innocent as you. Besides, I thank you for being a good sign. When a king has fallen so low that rats make a bed of him, his luck only can get better."

He got up, stepped out of the stall, and heard children's voices. The barn door opened and two little girls entered. As soon as they saw him, they stopped talking and stood still, looking at him with interest. After whispering together, they came closer and stopped again to gaze and whisper. By and by, they began to discuss him aloud. One said, "He has a handsome face."

The other added, "And pretty hair."

"But his clothes are poor."

"And he looks starved."

They came nearer, shyly circling and examining him as if he were some strange new animal who might bite. Finally they stopped in front of him, holding each other's hands for protection, and took a good satisfying look. Then one of them plucked up her courage and asked, "Who are you, boy?"

"I am the king" was the grave answer.

The children gave a little start, and their eyes opened wide. Then curiosity broke the silence. "The king? What king?"

"The king of England."

The children looked with wonder at each other, then at the king, then at each other again. One said, "Did you hear him, Margery? He said he is the king. Can that be true?"

"How can it be anything but true, Prissy? If it were not true, it would be a lie. And why would he lie?"

It was a good, tight argument. Prissy considered a moment, then tested the king with the simple remark, "If you truly are the king, then I believe you."

"I truly am the king."

That settled the matter. The two little girls asked him how he came to be where he was, why he was so plainly dressed, where he was going, and all about his business. Relieved to be treated with such honest concern, he told his tale with feeling, even forgetting his hunger. The little maids listened with sympathy. But when they learned how long the king had been without food, they cut him short and hurried him to the farmhouse for some breakfast.

The king was happy now and thought, "When I am restored to the throne, I always will honor little children, remembering how these girls believed in me in my time of trouble while adults made fun of me."

The children's mother received the king kindly and was touched by his troubled mind and poor rags. She was a widow and rather poor. Consequently, she felt sympathy for the unfortunate. Thinking that the boy, demented, had wandered away from his friends or caregivers; she tried to find out where he had been so that she could return him. But the king did not recognize any of the towns she mentioned. He spoke earnestly about court matters and broke down, more than once, when speaking of the late king his "father." Whenever the topic turned ordinary, he lost interest and became silent.

The woman was puzzled, but she did not give up. As she cooked, she tried to trick the boy into betraying his secret. She talked about cattle, then about sheep, but he showed no interest. She talked about millers, weavers, tinkers, blacksmiths, and other tradespeople. She mentioned mental hospitals, jails, and charity houses. Eventually she narrowed the field to domestic service. He must have been a house servant, she thought. But the subjects of building a fire, sweeping, scrubbing, and washing failed to interest him. Then she introduced the subject of cooking. The king's face lit up. "Ah, I have found him out. He worked in a kitchen," she thought. She stopped talking and let the king, inspired by a growing hunger and the good smells that came from the stove, ramble on about his favorite foods. He kept talking, discussing numerous dishes eaten only by the rich. "He must have worked in the king's own kitchen," the woman thought. To test her theory, she asked the king to watch the food cooking on the stove a moment, hinting that he might make a dish or two if he chose. Then she left the room and signaled her children to follow.

The king's intentions were good, but he soon fell into deep thought about royal business, and the food burned. The woman returned in time to save the breakfast from total destruction. She scolded the king but immediately softened when she saw how troubled he was over his mistake.

The boy ate a satisfying meal. Both sides disregarded the other's rank. The woman had intended to feed this young beggar scraps in a corner, like any other tramp, but she was so sorry about the scolding she had given him that she allowed him to sit at the family table. The king, in turn, was so remorseful about having burned the meal that he punished himself by eating with the family instead of requiring that the woman and her children wait on him. The widow felt pleased with her generosity to a tramp, and the king complimented himself for being humble with a peasant.

When the king was about to leave the widow's house to continue his journey, he spotted John Canty, with a peddler's pack on his back, and Hugo approaching the front gate. To avoid being seen by them, he slipped out the back way.

CHAPTER 20

The King and the Hermit

A high hedge hid the king from view as he raced toward a forest in the distance. He didn't slow down until he was deep in the woods. Then he stopped, thinking that he was safe. He listened intently. His straining ear detected sounds, but they were far away.

The king wanted to rest, but he had to keep moving to stay warm. Hoping to find a road, he went straight through the forest. He traveled on and on, but the farther he went, the denser the trees became. The gloom began to thicken, and he realized that night was coming on. The thought of spending the night in such a strange place made him shudder. He tried to go faster, but he could not see well enough. He kept tripping over roots and tangling himself in vines and thorns.

How glad he was when he finally saw a light's glimmer! He approached it warily, frequently stopping to look around and listen. The light came from a window in a hut. The king heard a voice and wanted to run and hide, but he immediately changed his mind when he realized that the voice was praying. He glided to the hut's window, raised himself on tiptoe, and looked inside. The room was small, with a dirt floor. In a corner was a bed of rushes with a ragged blanket. Nearby were a pail, a cup, a basin, and two or three pots and pans. There was a short bench with a three-legged stool. The remains of a fire smoldered on the hearth. An aged man knelt before a shrine lit by a single candle. An open book and a human skull lay on an old wooden box at his side. The man had a large, bony frame. His hair and whiskers were very long and snowy white, and he wore a sheepskin robe that reached from his neck to his heels.

"A holy hermit," the king said to himself. "I am indeed fortunate."

The hermit rose from his knees, and the king knocked. A deep voice responded, "Enter, but leave sin behind; the ground where you will stand is holy." The king entered and paused. The hermit turned a pair of gleaming eyes on him and asked, "Who are you?"

"I am the king," the boy answered with peaceful simplicity.

"Welcome, king!" the hermit cried with enthusiasm. Bustling about in feverish activity and repeatedly saying "welcome," he threw some twigs onto the fire, seated the king at his bench, and started to pace. "Welcome! Many people have sought sanctuary here. They were unworthy, so I turned them away. But a king who throws his crown aside, despises his life's vain riches, and dresses in rags to devote his life to holiness and physical discipline—he is worthy and welcome. He will live here for the rest of his life."

The king started to explain, but the hermit continued talking, with a louder voice and more energy. "No one will discover you or disturb you with their requests to return to that empty and foolish life that God told you to abandon," the hermit said. "You will pray here and study the Bible. You will meditate on the foolishness of this world and the beauty of the world to come. You will drink only water, eat crusts and herbs, and punish your body with daily whipping, to purify your soul." Still pacing, the old man stopped speaking aloud and started to mutter. The king seized this opportunity to state his case, but the hermit interrupted, "Sh. I will tell you a secret." Putting his face close to the king's, he whispered, "I am an archangel."

The king started violently and thought, "I wish I were with the outlaws again. Now I am the prisoner of a madman!" His face was full of fear.

The hermit continued in a low, excited voice. "There's awe in your face. I see that you feel my presence. Five years ago, on this very spot, angels sent from heaven made me an archangel. They knelt to me! They knelt to me because I am greater than they are. I have walked in heaven's courts and seen God face to face." He paused. Suddenly his face changed, and he said angrily, "I am a mere archangel. Twenty years ago, in a dream from heaven, I was told that I was to be pope. But the king dissolved the religious house where I was a monk. Robbed of my destiny, I was left poor, friendless,

and homeless." Beating his forehead with his fist, he raged, "Now I am nothing but an archangel, when I should have been pope!" He went on like this for an hour while the poor king sat and suffered.

Suddenly the hermit's voice softened and he spoke simply and sweetly. He moved the king nearer to the fire and made him comfortable. With a deft hand, he tended to the king's scrapes and bruises. Then he prepared supper, chatting pleasantly the whole time. Occasionally he gently patted his visitor's head. The boy lost his fear, and the two had a pleasant supper.

After a prayer before the shrine, the hermit put the boy to bed in a small adjoining room, tucking him in as snugly and lovingly as a mother might. Then he sat by the fire and began to poke at the smoldering wood. Pausing, he tapped his forehead several times with his fingers as if trying to remember something. Then he jumped from his seat, entered his guest's room, and asked, "You are a king?"

"Yes," the king answered drowsily.

"Which king?"

"Of England."

"Of England. Then, Henry is gone."

"Alas, yes. I am his son."

A harsh frown settled on the hermit's face, and he clenched his bony hands with vengeful energy. He stood a few moments, breathing fast and swallowing repeatedly. Then he said in a husky voice, "Henry was the one who made me homeless." There was no response. The king was asleep. The hermit bent down and looked at the boy. An expression of evil satisfaction replaced his frown. Dreaming, the king briefly smiled. "He is content," the hermit muttered, turning away.

Continuing to mutter, he started searching his

hut. Finally, he found what he was looking for: a rusty butcher knife and a whetstone. He sat at his bench and, still muttering, began to sharpen the knife on the stone. The wind sighed around the lonely hut, and the night's mysterious voices floated past. From cracks in the walls, the shining eyes of mice and rats peered at the old man. Sometimes he drew his thumb along the knife's edge and nodded with satisfaction. "It's getting sharper," he said. He worked calmly, occasionally speaking to himself. "His father destroyed me and has gone down into the eternal fires. His father ruined me. I am only an archangel. If it weren't for him, I would be pope."

The king stirred. The hermit sprang noiselessly to the bedside and went down onto his knees, bending over the boy with his knife uplifted. The boy stirred again and opened his eyes for a moment, but he saw nothing. The next moment he again slept soundly. The hermit watched and listened for a while, keeping still and scarcely breathing. Then he slowly lowered his arm and crept away, saying, "It is long past midnight. He might cry out and be heard by a passerby." He glided about his hut, gathering rags and rope. Then he returned and managed to tie the king's ankles together without waking him. Next he tied his wrists. Finally, he wrapped a bandage under the sleeper's chin and up over his head and tied it tight. This was all done so slowly and softly that the boy slept through it without stirring.

CHAPTER 21

Hendon to the Rescue

The old man glided away and then returned, bringing his bench. He sat, with half his body in the flickering light and the other half in shadow. He stared at the boy while softly sharpening his knife, and mumbled and chuckled. After a long time, he suddenly observed that the boy's eyes were wide open, staring in frozen horror at the knife. Smiling with satisfaction, the hermit asked, "Son of Henry the Eighth, have you prayed?"

The boy struggled helplessly in his bonds and forced a smothered sound through his closed jaws, which the hermit took as a positive response.

"Then, pray again. Pray the prayer for the dying."

The boy shuddered, and his face paled. Turning and twisting, he again struggled to free himself. He tugged frantically but could not loosen his bonds.

Calmly sharpening his knife, the hermit smiled, nodded, and mumbled, "Your remaining moments are precious and few. Pray the prayer for the dying."

The boy groaned and stopped struggling. Tears trickled down his face.

This did not soften the old man. He saw the dawn coming and spoke nervously. "I cannot enjoy this pleasure any longer. The night already is gone. Son of the Church's spoiler, close your dying eyes if you are afraid to look." The old man sank to his knees and, holding the knife, bent over the moaning boy.

But then they both heard voices. The knife dropped from the hermit's hand. He threw a sheepskin over the boy and jumped up, trembling. The voices grew louder. They were rough and angry. Then came blows, cries for help, and a clatter of swiftly retreating footsteps. Immediately there were thunderous knocks at door, followed by "Hello? Open! Come quickly, in the name of all the devils!" Oh, this was the best sound that the king ever had heard. It was Miles Hendon's voice!

Grinding his teeth in rage, the hermit swiftly left the bedchamber. He closed the door behind him. The king soon heard Hendon say, "Homage and greeting, reverend sir! Where is the boy?"

"What boy, friend?"

"What boy? Do not try to deceive me, priest. Near here I caught the scoundrels who stole him from me, and I made them confess. They said that he was on his own again and that they had tracked him to your door. They showed me his footprints. Delay no more. Where is the boy?"

"Oh, good sir, perhaps you mean the ragged royal vagrant who stayed the night here. I have sent him on an errand. He will return soon."

"How soon? Can I overtake him? How soon will he be back?"

"You don't need to chase him. He will return quickly."

"I will stay here until he returns, then. Wait a minute. You say that you sent him on an errand. That's a lie. He wouldn't go. He would pull your old beard if you told him to run an errand. You have lied. He would not go for you or any other man."

"For any man, no. But I am not a man."

"What? What are you, then?"

"I am an archangel."

"What?... What noise was that?"

Trembling with both fear and hope, the king had been groaning as loudly as he could, trying to get Hendon to hear him. Now he tried again, with all his energy, just as the hermit said, "Noise? I heard only the wind."

"Maybe. I have been hearing it faintly the whole time. There it is again. It isn't the wind."

The king's hope intensified. His tired lungs did their best, but his sealed jaws and the muffling sheepskin kept him from being effective. His heart sank when he heard the hermit say, "It came from outside, from the thicket. Come. I'll lead the way."

The king heard the two leave, talking. Their footsteps quickly died away. Then he was alone with an awful silence. It seemed ages until he heard the steps and voices approaching again. This time he also heard the trampling of hoofs. And he heard Hendon say, "I won't wait any longer. I can't. He has lost his way in this thick wood. Which direction did he take? Quickly. Point it out to me."

"He... Wait. I'll go with you."

"Good. You are better than you look. I don't think there's another archangel with a heart as good as yours. Will you take the little donkey that I brought for my boy, or will you put your holy legs over this bad-tempered mule that I have provided for myself?"

"Ride your mule, and lead your donkey. I am surer on my feet."

"Then, please mind the little donkey for me while I take my life in my hands and try to mount this big mule." A confusion of kicks, cuffs, tramplings, and falls followed, accompanied by thunderous curses and finally a bitter word to the mule. This must have broken the mule's spirit because the hostilities stopped.

With despair the captive king heard the voices and footsteps fade away. "My only friend has been deceived and gotten rid of," he thought. "The hermit will return and..." He began to struggle so frantically that he shook off the smothering sheepskin.

He heard the door open. The sound chilled him to the bone. He seemed to feel the knife at his throat. But the next moment, John Canty and Hugo stood before him. If his jaws had been free, he would have exclaimed, "Thank God!" A moment or two later, his limbs were untied and his captors, each gripping him by an arm, were hurrying him through the forest.

CHAPTER 22

A Victim of Treachery

Once more the king was roving with tramps and outlaws, the object of their rude jokes and sometimes, when the Ruffler's back was turned, the victim of Canty's and Hugo's spite. Only Canty and Hugo really disliked him. Some of the others liked him, and all admired his pluck and spirit.

All of the gang's attempts to get the king to steal failed. On the day of his return, he was sent into an unguarded kitchen. Instead of stealing something, he tried to warn the residents. Hugo took the king to beg in the company of a ragged woman and diseased baby, but the king neither begged nor helped the others in any way. Finding his tramping life almost unbearable, he always was trying to escape.

For two or three days Hugo, who was in charge of the king, tried to make the boy uncomfortable. At night, during the group's parties, he amused everyone by lightly injuring the king as if by accident. Twice he stepped on the king's toes "accidentally." The king, behaving royally, ignored this. But the third time that Hugo did it, the king knocked him to the ground with a heavy stick, to

the tribe's delight. Hugo sprang up, seized a stick, and came at his small enemy in a fury. Instantly a ring formed around the warriors, and betting and cheering began. But Hugo stood no chance. His frantic, clumsy efforts were no match for an arm trained by Europe's masters in every art and trick of swordsmanship. The little king stood, alert but gracefully relaxed, and turned aside the thick rain of blows with an ease and precision that made the onlookers wild with admiration. Every now and then, when his practiced eye saw an opening and he gave a lightning-swift rap to Hugo's head, cheers and laughter swept the place. After fifteen minutes Hugo—battered, bruised, and the target of ridicule—slunk away. The joyous rabble lifted the fight's unwounded hero onto their shoulders. With great ceremony they crowned him King of the Gamecocks. The gang solemnly canceled his lower title of Foo-Foo the First and vowed to exile anyone who dared to use it.

The next morning, Hugo awoke with a vengeful heart. He devised a plot to humiliate the king. He would put a fake wound on the king's leg. Then he would force the king to expose his leg in the highway and beg for money. He would create the fake wound by spreading a paste of lime powder, soap, and iron rust on a piece of leather that he then would bind tightly to the king's leg. The skin would absorb this mixture and peal off, leaving raw, red flesh. Next he would rub blood onto the leg. When dry, the blood would give the leg a dark, repulsive color. Finally he would apply a bandage of soiled rags in a cleverly careless way that would allow passersby to see the hideous ulcer and would arouse their sympathy.

Hugo got the help of the tinker, whom the king once had threatened with a soldering iron. They took the boy out as if for some tinkering jobs. As soon as they were out of sight of the camp, they threw him down. The tinker held him while Hugo tightly bound the paste to his leg. The king raged and promised to hang them the moment the scepter was in his hand again. But they kept a firm grip on him and laughed at his struggling and threats. The poultice soon began to bite. But then the "slave" who had made the speech denouncing England's laws appeared on the scene and put an end to the business, removing the bandage and poultice. The king wanted to borrow his rescuer's stick and beat the two rascals. The man, however, said no; he didn't want to attract the authorities. The rescuer marched the party back to camp and reported the incident to the Ruffler, who listened and pondered.

The Ruffler decided to reassign the king, from begging to stealing. Hugo was overjoyed. He already had tried, and failed, to make the king steal, but he thought that the king would obey the Ruffler. Hugo planned a raid for that very afternoon. He intended to betray the king so that he would be arrested.

When the time came, Hugo and the king walked to a neighboring village. Slowly they drifted up and down one street after another. Hugo looked for a chance to achieve his evil purpose. The king looked for a chance to escape. Hugo's chance came first: he spotted a woman carrying a basket holding a large bundle. His eyes sparkled as he thought, "I'll put this crime on the King of the Gamecocks." Excitedly, he waited and watched. When the woman started to pass them, Hugo told the king, "Wait here until I come back," and darted stealthily after his prey.

The king was overjoyed. He could escape now

if Hugo's task carried him far enough away. But he had no such luck. Hugo crept behind the woman, snatched her bundle, and came running back, wrapping it in an old piece of blanket that he carried on his arm. The woman felt, but did not see, the bundle being taken. Hugo quickly thrust the bundle into the king's hands. "Cry 'Stop! Thief!' he told the king, "and lead the crowd away from me by running in another direction." The next moment, Hugo turned a corner and darted down a crooked alley. A few seconds later he walked into view again, looking innocent and indifferent, and took up a position behind a post to watch what would happen.

Insulted, the king threw the bundle onto the ground. The blanket opened just as the woman arrived, with a growing crowd at her heels. She seized the king's wrist with one hand, snatched up her bundle with the other, and poured a stream of abuse onto the boy.

Hugo had seen enough. His enemy was captured; the law would get him now. So he slipped away, chuckling, and headed toward camp.

Struggling to free himself from the woman's grip, the king cried, "Unhand me, you foolish creature! I'm not the one who took your goods."

The crowd closed in, threatening the king and calling him names. A brawny blacksmith, in a leather apron and sleeves rolled to his elbows, reached for him, saying that he would beat him to teach him a lesson.

Just then a long sword flashed in the air and fell with convincing force on the man's arm, flat side down. Its owner remarked pleasantly, "Good souls, let's proceed gently, not with hostility and mean words. This is a matter for the law. Let the boy go, good woman."

With a glance the blacksmith sized up the strong soldier; he left, muttering and rubbing his arm. The woman reluctantly released the boy's wrist. The crowd gave the stranger dirty looks but kept their mouths shut. With flushed cheeks and sparking eyes, the king sprang to his rescuer's side, exclaiming, "You took a while, but you came just at the right time, Sir Miles. Carve this crowd to ribbons!"

CHAPTER 23

The King as a Prisoner

Hendon forced back a smile, bent down, and whispered into the king's ear, "Be quiet, my king. Trust in me, and all will go well." Then he added to himself, "'Sir Miles.' Bless me, I had forgotten that I am a knight. How well he remembers his quaint and crazy fantasies! My title is empty and foolish, but it is worth something. I think it is more honorable to be a ghost knight in his Kingdom of Dreams and Shadows than to be an earl in some of this world's real kingdoms."

The crowd parted to admit a constable, who approached and was about to lay his hand on the king's shoulder when Hendon said, "Gently, good friend. Withhold your hand. He will go peaceably; I am responsible for that. Lead on. We will follow."

The officer led, with the woman and her bundle close behind. Hendon and the king followed, with the crowd at their heels. The king wanted to rebel, but Hendon quietly said, "Think about it, sire. Your laws are the product of your own royalty. Will you reject them, yet require your subjects to respect them? Apparently, one of these laws has been broken."

"You are right. You will see that whatever the king of England requires a subject to suffer under the law, he himself will suffer while he holds the rank of a subject."

When the woman was called to testify before the justice of the peace, she swore that the small prisoner at the bar was the person who had committed the theft. No one could prove her wrong, so the king stood convicted. The bundle now was unrolled. When the contents proved to be a butchered piglet, the judge looked troubled. Hendon paled. Protected by his ignorance, the king had no reaction. The judge meditated, then turned to the woman and asked, "What is this property worth?"

The woman curtsied and replied, "Three shillings and eight pence, your worship. Not a penny less."

The justice glanced around uncomfortably at the crowd, then said to the constable, "Clear the court and close the doors."

It was done. No one remained but the two officials, the accused, the accuser, and Hendon.

The judge turned to the woman and said, "He's a poor, ignorant lad who perhaps was driven by hunger. These are hard times for the unfortunate. He doesn't have an evil face. When hunger... Good woman, do you know that when someone steals something worth more than thirteen pence and a half penny, the law says that he will hang for it?"

The king started but controlled himself and held his tongue. The woman sprang to her feet and cried, "God have mercy! I would not hang the poor thing. What should I do? What *can* I do?"

The justice said calmly, "You can change the value. I have not recorded it yet."

"Then, in God's name, say that the pig cost only eight pence."

In his delight, Hendon forgot all dignity and embarrassed the king by hugging him.

The woman said a grateful goodbye and started away with her piglet. After opening the door for her, the constable followed her out into the hall.

The justice proceeded to write in his record book.

Hendon, always alert, wanted to know why the constable had followed the woman out, so he slipped out into the hall and listened. He heard the constable say, "It is a fat piglet and promises good eating. I will buy it from you. Here is eight pence."

"Eight pence, indeed! It cost me three shillings and eight pence. A fig for your eight pence."

"So, you swore falsely when you said that the value was only eight pence. Come back inside with me and tell the judge."

"Say no more. Give me the eight pence, and be quiet about the matter." The woman went off crying.

Hendon slipped back into the courtroom, and the constable followed after hiding his prize in a convenient place.

The justice wrote a while longer, then read the king a wise and kindly lecture. He sentenced the king to a short imprisonment in the common jail, to be followed by a public flogging.

The astounded king opened his mouth and probably was going to order the good judge to be beheaded on the spot, but he caught a warning sign from Hendon and closed his mouth before anything slipped out. Hendon took the king by the hand and bowed to the judge, and the two followed the constable toward the jail. The moment they reached the street, the angry monarch halted, snatched away his hand, and exclaimed to Hendon, "Idiot, do you imagine that I will enter a common jail?"

Hendon bent down and said somewhat sharply, "Peace! Don't hurt our chances by saying anything dangerous. Wait and be patient. Trust me."

CHAPTER 24

The Escape

The short winter day was nearly over. The streets were deserted except for a few stragglers, who hurried on their errands and paid no attention to the king, Hendon, and the constable. Edward the Sixth wondered if the sight of a king on his way to jail had ever before encountered such indifference.

Soon the group arrived at a deserted market square. When they were halfway across it, Hendon laid his hand on the constable's arm and said in a low voice, "Wait a moment, sir. There is no one here to hear, and I want to say something."

"My duty forbids it, sir. Please don't hinder me. It's getting dark."

"The matter concerns you. Turn your back a moment, and pretend not to see. Let this poor lad escape."

"You dare say this to me? I arrest you in..."

"Don't be hasty," Hendon said. Then he whispered, "The piglet that you bought for eight pence may cost you your neck."

At first the constable was speechless. Then he began to threaten.

Hendon waited patiently until he was done. Then he said, "I heard every word you said to the woman." He repeated, word for word, the hallway conversation between the constable and the woman. "There. Won't I be able to tell it correctly to the judge, if necessary?"

For a moment the man was silent with fear. Then he said with forced lightness, "It's making much out of a joke. I only teased the woman for my amusement."

"Did you keep the woman's piglet for amusement?"

The man answered sharply, "Yes. I tell you it was only a jest."

"Wait here while I run and ask the judge what he thinks of your jest."

The constable hesitated, then said, "The judge has no more sense of humor than a corpse. I seem to be in a fix because of an innocent pleasantry. I am a family man, and my wife and little ones... What do you want of me?"

"Only that you stand here seeing nothing while counting slowly to a hundred thousand."

"That would be my destruction," the constable said with distress. "Be reasonable, good sir. Even if my buying the piglet wasn't a joke, the judge would punish me with more than a warning."

Hendon replied with a seriousness that chilled the air around him. "The law has a name for this joke of yours. Do you know what it is?"

"Sweet heaven, I never dreamed it had a name."

"In the law this crime is called 'non compos mentis lex talionis sic transit gloria mundi.'"

"Oh!"

"The penalty is death."

"God have mercy!"

"You took advantage of someone who was at *your* mercy. You paid only a trifle for goods worth more than thirteen pence. This, in the eyes of the law, is constructive barratry, misprision of treason, and ad hominem expurgatis in status quo. The penalty is death by the noose, without the benefit of a priest."

"Hold me up, good sir. My legs do fail me. Spare me this doom, and I will turn my back and see nothing."

"Good. You now are being wise and reasonable. And you will return the piglet?"

"I will, indeed. Go. I will say that you broke into the jailhouse and took the prisoner from my hands by force. The jailhouse door is old. I will batter it down myself between midnight and morning."

"Do it, good soul. No harm will come of it. The judge feels charity for this poor lad and will shed no tears and break no jailer's bones over his escape."

CHAPTER 25

Hendon Hall

As soon as Hendon and the king were out of the constable's sight, his majesty was instructed to hurry to a certain place outside the town and wait there while Hendon settled his account at the inn. Half an hour later the two friends were happily jogging eastward on Hendon's pitiful steeds. The king was warm and comfortable now because he had taken off his rags and put on the secondhand suit that Hendon had bought on London Bridge.

Hendon did not want to tire the boy out. He thought that hard journeys, irregular meals, and little sleep would be bad for his crazed mind, whereas rest, regularity, and moderate exercise would hasten its cure. He longed to see the boy lose his diseased visions and become healthy again. Therefore, he decided to move toward his home in easy stages rather than give in to his impatience and hurry along day and night.

When he and the king had traveled about ten miles, they reached a sizeable village. They stayed there for the night at a good inn. The old customs resumed. Hendon waited on the king and stood behind his chair while he dined. Hendon also undressed the king when he was ready for bed.

Then he slept on the floor in front of the door, rolled up in a blanket.

The next day and the day after that, they jogged lazily along, talking about their adventures and greatly enjoying each other's stories.

Hendon described his wide wanderings in search of the king and how the hermit had led him a fool's journey all over the forest. The hermit finally had taken Hendon back to the hut, when he had found that he could not get rid of him. Then the old man had gone into the bed chamber and come staggering back looking broken-hearted, saying that he had expected to find the boy there, resting from his errand, but it was not so. Hendon had waited at the hut all day. Hope of the king's return had died out then, and he had left to resume his search. "And old Sanctum Sanctorum was truly sorry your highness did not come back," Hendon said. "I saw it in his face."

"I don't doubt that," the king said. Then he told his own story, after which Hendon was sorry that he had not killed the hermit.

During the trip's last day, Hendon's spirits soared. He talked constantly. He chatted about his father and his brother Arthur, telling stories that showed their noble and generous characters. He went into loving frenzies over his Edith and was so glad-hearted that he even was able to say some gentle and brotherly things about Hugh. He dwelt on the coming meeting at Hendon Hall. What a surprise it would be to everyone, and what an outburst of thanksgiving and delight there would be.

It was pretty country, dotted with cottages and orchards. The road led through broad pastures whose dips and crests looked like waves. Hendon often strayed from his course to a nearby hill, hoping he might catch a glimpse of his home. At last he succeeded and cried excitedly, "There is the village, my king, and there is the Hall close by! You can see the towers from here. That forest is my father's park. Ah, now you will know what grandeur is. A house with seventy rooms—think of that. Twenty-seven servants. A fancy lodging for the likes of us, no? Come, let us hurry. My impatience won't tolerate any more delay."

They traveled as fast as they could. Still, it was after three o'clock before they reached the village. They scampered through it. Hendon chattered the entire time. "Here is the church, covered with the same ivy. There is the inn, the old Red Lion. Over there is the marketplace. Here is the Maypole. Nothing has changed—nothing except the people, that is. Ten years changes people. I know some of these people, but no one knows me."

When they reached the end of the village, they entered a crooked, narrow road lined with tall hedges. They hurried down this road for half a mile. Then they passed through an imposing stone gateway carved with coats of arms, into a vast flower garden. A noble mansion lay before them.

"Welcome to Hendon Hall, my king!" Hendon exclaimed. "It's a great day. My father and my brother and Lady Edith will be so mad with joy that they will have eyes only for me at first, so you will feel coldly welcomed. But that will change. When I say that you are my ward and tell them how much I care for you, they'll take you in their arms for my sake, and you'll make Hendon Hall your home forever."

Hendon sprang to the ground before the great door, helped the king down, took him by the hand, and rushed inside. They entered a spacious apartment. Hendon sat the king down and ran toward a young man who sat at a writing table in front of a log fire. "Embrace me, Hugh!" he cried. "Say that you are glad I have returned. Call our father. Home is not home until I touch his hand, see his face, and hear his voice."

Hugh drew back and stared at Miles. He looked offended. Then his expression changed to curiosity mixed with compassion. He said in a mild voice, "Your wits seem touched, poor stranger. No doubt you have suffered greatly at the world's hands. Your appearance shows it. Who do you believe me to be?"

"Believe? I believe you to be the person you *are*: Hugh Hendon," Miles said sharply.

Hugh continued in a soft tone, "And who do you imagine that *you* are?"

"Imagination has nothing to do with it! Do you pretend that you don't recognize your own brother, Miles Hendon?"

A look of pleased surprise flitted across

Hugh's face. "What? Can the dead come back to life? God be praised if it is so. Our poor lost boy back in our arms after all these years? Quick! Come to the light. Let me look at you." He seized Miles by the arm, dragged him to the window, and examined him from head to foot, turning him this way and that and walking around him.

Meanwhile Miles smiled, laughed, and kept nodding his head. "Go on, brother. Inspect me as you like. Dear Hugh, I am indeed Miles, your lost brother." He was about to embrace his brother when Hugh put up his hand to stop him.

Mournfully, Hugh dropped his chin and said, "God give me the strength to bear this disappointment."

Amazed, Miles was speechless. Then he cried, "What disappointment?"

Shaking his head sadly, Hugh said, "I pray to heaven that other people will see the resemblance that I cannot. I fear that the letter spoke the truth."

"What letter?"

"One that came from overseas six or seven years ago. It said that my brother Miles had died in battle."

"It was a lie! Call Father. He will know me."

"I cannot call the dead."

"Dead?" Miles's lips trembled. "My father dead? This is grievous news. Please let me see my brother Arthur. He will know me."

"He also is dead."

"God be merciful! Dead? My father and

Arthur both dead? Do not say that Lady Edith..."

"Is dead? No."

"God be praised for that! Hurry, brother. Call her here. She will know me. Call the old servants, too. They, too, will know me."

"Only five of the old servants still are here at the Hall: Peter, Halsey, David, Bernard, and Margaret." So saying, Hugh left the room.

Miles stood musing. Then he paced. "The five villains still are here but none of the twenty-two honest servants," he muttered. He had forgotten all about the king.

After a while his majesty said gravely, with genuine compassion, "I feel for you, good man. I know what it is to claim an identity that others deny."

"Ah, my king," Hendon cried, "I am no impostor. Lady Edith will confirm the truth of my identity. You will hear it from the sweetest lips in England. I know this old hall, these pictures of my ancestors, and all these things around us as a child knows its own nursery. I was born and bred here, my lord. Even if no one else believes me—I beg you—do not doubt me. I could not bear it."

"I do not doubt you," the king said with childlike faith and simplicity.

"I thank you from my heart!" Hendon exclaimed.

With the same gentle simplicity, the king said, "Do you doubt *me*?"

Hendon felt guilty confusion. He was grateful that Hugh entered at that moment, sparing him

the necessity of replying. A beautiful lady, richly clothed, followed Hugh, and several uniformed servants came after her. The lady walked slowly, with her head bowed and her eyes fixed on the floor. Her face was unspeakably sad. Miles sprang forward, crying, "Edith, my darling!"

Hugh waved him back and said to the lady, "Look at him. Do you know him?"

At the sound of Miles's voice the woman had started slightly, and her cheeks had flushed. She was trembling now. She stood still, during a pause of several moments. Then she slowly lifted her head and looked into Miles's eyes with a stony and frightened gaze. Her face paled. In a dead voice, she said, "I do not know him." Then she turned and, with a stifled sob, staggered out of the room.

Miles sank into a chair and covered his face with his hands.

After a pause, Hugh said to the servants, "You have observed him. Do you know him?" They shook their heads. "The servants do not know you, sir. I fear that there is some mistake. You have seen that my wife, too, did not recognize you."

"Your wife!" In an instant Miles pinned Hugh to the wall, gripping him by the throat. "You scoundrel! I see it all. You wrote the lying letter yourself, so that you could steal my bride and goods. Leave. Otherwise I will disgrace myself by killing you."

Red-faced and almost suffocated, Hugh reeled to the nearest chair and commanded the servants to seize and bind the murderous stranger.

They hesitated. "He is armed, Sir Hugh, and we are weaponless," one of them said.

"Armed? What difference does it make when there are so many of you? On him, I say!"

"You know me from before," Miles warned them. "I have not changed. Come at me if you dare."

The servants held back.

"Then go, you weak cowards," Hugh said. "Arm yourselves and guard the doors while I send someone for law officers." He turned at the doorway and said to Miles, "You'll be better off if you don't try to escape."

"Escape? You needn't worry about that. I am master of Hendon Hall and all its belongings. I intend to stay."

CHAPTER 26

Disowned

The king sat thinking a few moments, then looked up and said, "It's very strange. I cannot figure it out."

"No, it is not strange, my liege. I know Hugh. He always has been a rascal."

"Oh, I wasn't referring to him, Sir Miles."

"To what, then? What is strange?"

"That the king is not missed."

"What? I do not understand."

"It is strange that the land is not filled with messengers and proclamations describing my person and searching for me. Is it not distressing that the head of state has vanished?"

"True, my king. I had forgotten." Miles sighed and thought, "Poor ruined mind, still busy with its pathetic dream."

"I have a plan that will set things right for both of us. I will write a paper in three tongues—Latin, Greek, and English—and you will take it to London in the morning. Give it to my uncle, Lord Hertford. When he sees it, he will know that I wrote it. Then he will send for me."

"Might it not be best, your majesty, for us to wait here until I prove myself and secure my right to my lands? Then I would be better able to..."

"Peace! What are your small lands compared to a nation's concerns and a throne's integrity?" Regretting his severity, the added gently, "Obey and have no fear. I will restore you. I will make you whole. More than whole. I will remember and repay you." He took the pen and set to work.

Miles watched him lovingly awhile, thinking, "He speaks like a true king. Where did he learn to do that? Look at him scratch away contentedly at his meaningless doodles, believing them to be Latin and Greek. If I can't figure out how to distract him, I will be forced to pretend to leave tomorrow on this wild errand that he has invented for me."

Miles's thoughts returned to recent events. When the king handed him what he had written, Miles pocketed it without even looking at it. "Why did Edith act as she did?" he wondered. "Surely, she recognized me, yet she claimed not to know me. Perhaps Hugh commanded her to lie. She seemed stricken with fear. Yes, she was under his influence. I will find her. Now that Hugh is away, she will speak her true mind. She will remember the old times when we were friends. She loved me in those days. She will tell the truth. She always was honest and true."

He stepped eagerly toward the door. At that moment it opened, and Lady Edith entered. Her face was very pale and as sad as before, but she walked with grace and dignity. Miles sprang forward to meet her, but she stopped him with a hardly perceptible gesture. She sat down and, with formality, asked him to do the same. "Sir, I have come to warn you," she said. "Mad people cannot be talked out of their false beliefs, but they may be persuaded to avoid danger. Do not stay here because it is dangerous." For a moment, she looked steadily into Miles's face. "It is even more dangerous because you resemble our lost boy if he had lived."

"Heavens, madam, I am he!"

"I truly think that you believe it, sir. I do not question your honesty. I only warn you. My husband is master in this region, and his power has hardly any limit. He will tell everyone that you are a mad impostor, and everyone will echo him." She gave Miles that steady look again. "If you were Miles Hendon, and he knew it and all the region knew it, he still would deny you and denounce you, and no one would be brave enough to acknowledge you."

"So it seems," Miles said bitterly. "Even a life-long friend has betrayed me."

The lady blushed and dropped her eyes to the floor. "You must leave. Otherwise my husband will destroy you. He is a tyrant and has no pity. Your claims endanger his title and possessions. You have assaulted him in his own house. Go without further delay. If you lack money, I beg you to take this purse and bribe the servants to let you pass. Escape while you can."

Miles declined the purse and rose from his

chair. "Grant me one thing," he said. "Look into my eyes. Now answer me. Am I Miles Hendon?"

"No. I do not know you."

"Swear it."

She answered in a low but distinct voice. "I swear."

"Oh, this is beyond belief!"

"Fly! Why do you waste precious time? Fly and save yourself!"

At that moment law officers burst into the room, and a violent struggle began. Miles soon was overpowered. Both he and the king were bound and taken to prison.

CHAPTER 27

In Prison

Because all of the cells were crowded, the two friends were chained in a large room where people charged with minor offenses usually were kept. There were about twenty handcuffed or chained men and women, of varying ages. It was a crude, noisy gang. The king was bitterly annoyed by this insult to his royal dignity. Hendon was silent. He had come home, a happy returning son, expecting to be greeted with joy. He was stunned by the difference between his expectations and reality.

Wrapped in soiled prison blankets, Hendon and the king spent a troubled night. For a bribe the jailer had given liquor to some of the prisoners. This resulted in dirty songs, fighting, and shouting. Some time after midnight a man attacked a woman. He nearly killed her by beating her over the head with his handcuffs before the jailer came to the rescue. The jailer soundly clubbed the man on his head and shoulders. Then the violence stopped. Everyone had a chance to sleep, if they could ignore the moans and groans of the two wounded people.

The next week passed without change. Men

whose faces Hendon remembered more or less distinctly came, by day, to gaze at the "impostor" and insult him. By night there was brawling.

Then the jailer brought in an old man and told him, "The villain is in this room. Look around and see if you can say which one he is."

Hendon glanced up and felt some happiness for the first time since he had been jailed. He thought, "This is Blake Andrews, a servant all his life in my father's family—a good, honest soul (at least, when I knew him)."

The old man gazed around the room, glancing at each face. Finally, he said, "I see no one here but petty criminals, scum of the streets. Which is he?"

The jailer laughed. "Here," he said. "Look at this big animal, and see what you think."

The old man approached and looked Hendon over, long and earnestly. Then he shook his head and said, "This is no Hendon!"

"Your old eyes still are good," the jailer said. "If I were Sir Hugh, I would take this rascal and..." The jailer finished by lifting himself on tiptoes with an imaginary noose while making a gurgling noise as if he were choking.

"Let him thank God if he fares any better," the old man said. "If it were up to me, he would roast."

"Give him a piece of your mind, old man," the jailer said. "You'll have fun." Then he left.

The old man dropped to his knees and whispered, "God be thanked, you have returned, my master! For seven years I believed that you were dead. Now here you are. I recognized you the moment that I saw you. It was hard work to keep a blank face and seem to see no one here but rubbish from the streets. I am old and poor, Sir Miles. But say the word, and I will go forth and proclaim the truth even if I am strangled for it."

"No," Hendon said. "It would ruin you and not help me. But I thank you for restoring my lost faith in my people."

The old servant became very valuable to Hendon and the king. He came several times a day to "abuse" the imposter and always smuggled in food. He also brought the current news. Hendon gave the food to the king because the boy couldn't eat the wretched food provided by the jailer. Andrews had to keep his visits short in order to avoid suspicion. But he managed to give Hendon quite a bit of information each time. He delivered his news in a low voice, for Hendon's benefit, and he delivered a few insults in a louder voice, for the benefit of others.

Little by little the family's story came out. Arthur had died six years ago. His death, in the absence of news from Miles, had worsened their father's health. Believing that he would die soon, Sir Richard had been eager for Hugh and Edith to marry. Hoping for Miles's return, Edith had begged for delay. Then the letter had come bringing news of Miles's death. The shock had devastated Sir Richard, and he and Hugh had insisted on the marriage. Edith had obtained a month's delay, then another, then another. Finally, the marriage had taken place at Sir Richard's deathbed. It had not been a happy one. It was whispered around the country that shortly after the wedding the bride had found, among her husband's papers, drafts of the letter announcing Miles's death. She had accused her husband of hastening their marriage, and Sir Richard's death, through wicked forgery. Tales of cruelty to Lady Edith and the servants were heard everywhere. Since his father's death, Hugh had dropped all of his disguises and become a pitiless master to everyone under his power.

At one point, Andrews remarked, "There is a rumor that the king is mad."

Glaring at the old man, the king said, "The king is not mad. You should mind your own business and not engage in this disloyal talk."

Surprised by this reaction, Andrews asked, "What does the lad mean?" Hendon gave him a sign, and Andrews did not pursue his question but continued with his update. "The late king is to be buried at Windsor in two days, on the sixteenth; the new king will be crowned at Westminster on the twentieth."

"I think they should find him first," his majesty muttered. Then he added confidently, "They will do that, and I will help them."

"In the name of..." A warning sign from Hendon stopped the old man's remark, and

Andrews resumed his gossip. "Sir Hugh will attend the coronation, with grand hopes. He expects to return with a title because he has favor with the Lord Protector."

"What Lord Protector?" his majesty asked.

"His grace the Duke of Somerset."

"What Duke of Somerset?"

"There is only one: Seymour, Earl of Hertford."

The king asked sharply, "Since when is he a duke and Lord Protector?"

"Since the last day of January."

"Who made him so?"

"He himself and the Great Council, with the help of the king."

His majesty started violently. "The king!" he cried. "What king, good sir?"

"What king, indeed! God have mercy, what ails the boy? Since we have only one, it is not difficult to answer: his most sacred majesty King Edward the Sixth, whom God preserve. He is a dear, sweet little waif. Whether or not he is mad—they say that he improves daily—his praises are on everyone's lips. All bless him and pray that he may reign long in England because he began humanely by saving the old Duke of Norfolk's life. Now he is bent on destroying the cruelest laws that oppress the people."

This news struck his majesty silent with amazement and sent him into such dismal thoughts that he heard no more of the old man's gossip. He wondered if the "little waif" was the beggar boy whom he had left dressed in his own garments in the palace. This did not seem possible. Surely the beggar boy's manners and speech would have betrayed him if he had pretended to be the Prince of Wales. He would have been driven out, and a search for the true prince would have begun. Could it be that the court had set up some noble as the new ruler? No, his uncle would not allow that. He was all-powerful and would crush such an attempt.

The boy's thoughts got him nowhere. The more he tried to solve the mystery, the more confused he became, the more his head ached, and the worse he slept. His impatience to get to London grew hourly, and his captivity became almost unbearable. Hendon's efforts to comfort him failed. But two women who were chained near the king did better. Under their gentle attention he found some peace. He was very grateful and came to love them. He asked them why they were in prison. When they said that they were Baptists, he smiled and asked, "Is that a crime worthy of prison? They will not keep you here long for such a little thing." The women did not answer. Something in their faces made the king uneasy. "You do not speak," he said, "Will there be some other punishment? Please tell me that there is no fear of that." They tried to change the topic, but he pressed on. "Will they whip you? Say that they will not."

The women betrayed confusion and distress. In a voice choked with emotion, one of them answered, "You break our hearts, gentle spirit. God will help us to bear our..."

The king broke in, "Then, they *are* going to whip you, the stony-hearted wretches. But you must not weep. I cannot bear it."

When the king awoke in the morning, the women were gone. "They have been released," he thought joyfully. Each of them had left a shred of ribbon pinned to his clothing, as a token of friendship. He told himself that he always would keep these things and that soon he would find these good friends and take them under his protection.

Just then the jailer came in with some guards and commanded that the prisoners go to the jail yard. The king was overjoyed. It would be a blessed thing to see the blue sky and breathe fresh air again. He was annoyed by the officers' slowness in unchaining the prisoners. At last, he and Hendon were unchained and ordered to follow the other prisoners.

The jail yard was paved with stone and open to the sky. The prisoners entered it through a massive stone archway and stood in a row with their backs against the wall. A rope was stretched in front of them and officers guarded them. It was a chill and overcast morning, and a light layer of snow whitened the great empty space and added to its general gloominess. Now and then a wintry wind shivered through the place and sent the snow flying.

In the yard's center stood two women, chained to posts. The king saw that these were his good friends. He shuddered and thought, "Alas, they have not been freed! To think that such people know the lash! In England! They will be whipped, and I, whom they have comforted and treated kindly, must watch this great wrong. I, the king, am helpless to protect them."

A great gate swung open, and a crowd of citizens poured in. They flocked around the two women and hid them from the king's view. A priest entered and passed through the crowd, and he too was hidden. The king heard talking back and forth, as if questions were being asked and answered, but he could not make out what was said. Next there was some bustle as officials passed through the crowd on the other side of the women. A hush fell over the people. By command the masses parted, and the king saw something that froze the marrow in his bones. Wood had been piled around the two women, and a kneeling man was lighting it! The women bowed their heads and covered their faces with their hands. Yellow flames began to climb upward through the crackling kindling, and wreaths of blue smoke streamed away on the wind. The clergyman lifted his hands and began a prayer.

Two young girls came flying through the great gate. With piercing screams, they threw themselves on the women at the stake. Officers tore them away. One of them was kept in a tight grip, but the other broke loose, saying that she would die with her mother. Once again she flung her arms around her mother's neck. She was torn away again, with her gown on fire. Two men held her, and the burning portion of her gown was ripped off and thrown aside. The whole time, she struggled to free herself, saying that she would be alone in the world now and begging to be allowed to die with her mother. Both girls continually screamed and fought for freedom.

Suddenly shrieks of agony drowned out this commotion. The king glanced from the frantic girls to the stake, then turned away and looked no more. "That image never will leave my memory," he thought. "I will see it every day and dream of it every night, until I die."

Hendon was watching the king. "His mental state is improving," he thought with satisfaction. "He has become gentler. If he had followed his impulse, he would have stormed at these villains, said that he was the king, and demanded that the women be released unharmed. Soon his delusion will disappear, and his mind will be whole again. God speed the day."

That same day several prisoners were brought in for the night. They were being shipped, under guard, to various places in the kingdom to receive punishment for their crimes. The king talked with these people, trying to instruct himself for his kingly duties. Their stories broke his heart. One of them was a poor, half-witted woman who had stolen a yard or two of cloth from a weaver. She was to be hanged for it. Another was a man found guilty of killing a deer in the king's park. He, too, was to be hanged. Another was a tradesman's apprentice sentenced to death for stealing a hawk. The youth had found the hawk after she escaped from her owner and, believing himself entitled to keep her, had taken her home with him.

The king was furious over these punishments and wanted Hendon to break out of jail and hurry with him to Westminster, so that he could mount his throne and save the lives of these unfortunate people. "Poor child," Hendon thought. "These woeful tales have worsened his illness."

Among the new prisoners was an old lawyer, a man with a strong face and a brave expression. Three years ago he had written a paper against the Lord Chancellor, accusing him of injustice. As punishment he had lost his law license and part of his ears; he also had been fined £3,000 and sentenced to life imprisonment. Recently he had repeated his offense and had been sentenced to pay a fine of £5,000, lose what remained of his ears, be branded on both cheeks, and remain in prison for life. "These are honorable scars," he said, pulling back his gray hair and showing the stubs that once had been his ears.

The king's eyes burned with passion. "Before the month is over, you will be free," he said. "The laws that have mistreated you, and shamed England, will be erased from the law books."

CHAPTER 28

The Sacrifice

When Miles's trial arrived, his claims to the Hendon honors and estates were completely ignored. He was sentenced to sit two hours in the public stocks for being a "vagabond" and for assaulting the master of Hendon Hall. On his way to punishment he raged and threatened. The officers dragged him roughly along and occasionally slapped him for outbursts. The king could not keep pace because of the crowd, so he followed at some distance. The king almost had been condemned to the stocks himself, for being in such bad company. But he had been set free with a lecture and a warning, in consideration of his youth.

When the crowd finally halted, the king ran excitedly around its edge, trying to get through. After much difficulty he succeeded. There sat his poor servant in the humiliating stocks, ridiculed by a dirty mob—he, the bodyguard of England's king! The king's anger turned into rage when he saw an egg sail through the air and break against Miles's cheek while the crowd roared with pleasure. He sprang across the open circle to the officer in charge. "For shame! This is my servant. Set him free. I am the..."

"Peace!" Miles exclaimed in a panic. "You will do yourself no good. Do not mind him, officer. He is mad."

"Do not worry about my minding him, good man; I have small mind to mind him. But I am inclined to teach him." The officer turned to a guard and said, "Give the little fool a taste or two of the lash, to teach him manners."

"Half a dozen would be better," Sir Hugh suggested, having ridden up a moment before to watch the proceedings.

The king was seized. He did not struggle, being paralyzed by the thought of the outrage about to be inflicted on his sacred person.

"Let the child go," Miles said. "Do you not see how young and frail he is? Let him go. I will take his lashes."

"What a good idea! Thanks for it," Hugh said with satisfaction. "Let the little beggar go, and give this fellow a dozen in his place—an honest dozen well laid on." The king was about to protest when Hugh silenced him with the threat, "Speak up. For each word that you say, he will get six more lashes."

Miles was removed from the stocks and his back uncovered. While the lash was applied, the king turned his face away and allowed unroyal tears to run down his cheeks. "Brave, good heart," he thought. "This loyal deed never will fade from my memory. In addition to saving your king from wounds and

possible death, you have performed an even greater service: you have saved him from shame."

Miles did not cry out under the lashing but bore the heavy blows with soldierly strength. This, together with his willingness to be whipped in place of the boy, commanded the respect of onlookers. The mob's shouting and hooting stopped. The only sound was the falling blows. The silence continued as Miles was put back into the stocks.

The king whispered into Miles's ear, "Kings cannot make you noble, you good, great soul. One who is higher than kings has done that already. But a king can confirm your nobility to men." He picked up the whip from the ground, lightly touched Miles's bleeding shoulders with it, and whispered, "Edward of England makes you earl."

Miles was touched. Tears welled in his eyes, and he said to himself, "Better these pretend dignities of mine—freely given by a good, clean spirit—than real ones bought by serving a corrupt power."

Hugh wheeled his horse around. As he galloped away, the living wall opened and then closed silently after his passage.

No one said anything in praise of the prisoner, but the absence of abuse was a sign of respect. Unaware of what had happened, a latecomer sneered at the "impostor" and prepared to throw a dead cat at him. He promptly was knocked down and kicked out. And the deep quiet returned.

CHAPTER 29

To London

When Hendon's time in the stocks ended, he was released and ordered to leave the region for good. His sword was given to him, and his mule and donkey. He mounted and rode off, followed by the king, the crowd opening with quiet respect to let them pass.

Hendon soon was absorbed in thought. What should he do? Where should he go? He must find powerful help or give up his inheritance and accept the disgrace of being an imposter. Where could he find this powerful help? After a while a possibility occurred to him. He remembered what old Andrews had said about the young king's goodness and his generous support of the wronged and unfortunate. Why not try to talk with the king and beg him for justice? But could a pauper gain admission to a monarch's great presence? Hendon determined to find a way. Yes, he would head for the capital. Maybe his father's old friend, Sir Humphrey Marlow, would help him: good old Sir Humphrey, Head Lieutenant of the late king's kitchen, or stables, or... Hendon could not remember just what or which. Now that he had a definite goal, the fog of humiliation and depression that had settled on his spirits lifted and blew away. He raised his head and looked around. He was surprised to see how far they had come. The village was far behind, and the king was jogging along in his wake, with his head bowed. He, too, was thinking and planning. A fear invaded Hendon's new cheerfulness. Would the boy be willing to return to a city where he never had known anything but hunger and abuse? The question must be asked. Hendon stopped his horse and called out, "I forgot to ask where we are going. Your command, my liege?"

"To London!"

Hendon moved on again, happy with the answer.

The journey proceeded without event, until the end. About ten o'clock on the night of February 19th, Hendon and the king arrived at London Bridge in the midst of a crowd of howling, cheering people whose beer-jolly faces shone in the glare of torches. Suddenly a former noble's decaying head, which had been displayed on a spike of the Bridge, tumbled down between them, striking Hendon on the elbow and falling into a jumble of feet. A citizen tripped over the fallen head and stumbled into someone in front of him, who then intentionally knocked down someone else and was himself laid flat by that person's friend. The time was ripe for a brawl because the festivities of the next day, Coronation Day, already were underway; everyone was full of strong drink. Within five minutes the brawl took up considerable ground; within ten or twelve, it covered an acre and had become a riot. By this time Hendon and the king were hopelessly separated from each other and lost in the crowd's turmoil.

CHAPTER 30

Tom's Progress

While the true king wandered around the land, poorly dressed, poorly fed, beaten and mocked by tramps, thrown into jail with thieves and murderers, and called idiot and impostor by almost everyone, the false king, Tom Canty, enjoyed quite a different experience.

When we last saw him, royalty was just beginning to have a bright side for him. This side became brighter every day. Within a very short time it became almost complete sunshine. He lost his fears and doubts. His embarrassments departed and were replaced by confidence. He made good use of the whipping boy's assistance. He ordered Lady Elizabeth and Lady Jane Grey into his presence whenever he wanted to play or talk and dismissed them when he was done with them. It no longer confused him to have these important people kiss his hand goodbye. He enjoyed being put to bed with complicated ceremony at night and dressed with equally elaborate ceremony in the morning. It was a pleasure to march to dinner attended by a glittering procession of officials and guards. Indeed, he liked it so much that he doubled his guards to a hundred. He liked to hear the bugles down the long hallways and the distant voices responding, "Make way for the king!" He enjoyed sitting on his throne during council and did more than just echo the Lord Protector's whispered instructions. He liked to receive great ambassadors and listen to the affectionate messages that they brought from distinguished monarchs who called him "brother." Oh, happy Tom Canty from Offal Court!

He enjoyed his splendid clothes and ordered more. He found his four hundred servants too few and tripled them. The adoration of bowing nobles was sweet to him. He remained kind and gentle and a determined defender of the oppressed, and he tirelessly fought unjust laws; however, when he was offended, he could turn on an earl, or even a duke, and give him a look that would make him tremble. Once, his royal "sister," self-righteous Lady Mary, argued against pardoning so many people who otherwise would be jailed, hanged, or burned. She reminded him that their late father's prisons sometimes had contained as many as 60,000 convicts and that he had ordered the execution of over 72,000 thieves and robbers. Angry, the boy ordered her to go to her room and ask God to replace the stone in her chest with a heart.

Did Tom ever feel troubled about the prince who had treated him so kindly and had run out with such passion to punish the guard who had beaten him? Yes. His first royal days and nights were filled with painful thoughts about the lost prince. He sincerely longed for his return to his rightful inheritance. But as time wore on, and the prince did not come, Tom's mind became busy with his new and enchanting experiences. Little by little the vanished monarch faded almost out of his thoughts. Eventually he was nothing more than an unwelcome ghost because the thought of him made Tom feel guilty and ashamed.

Tom's poor mother and sisters traveled the same road out of his mind. At first he cried for them and longed to see them. But later the thought of their arriving in rags and dirt, betraying him with their kisses, and dragging him back to poverty and despair made him shudder. Finally, to his relief, they nearly stopped troubling his thoughts. Whenever their mournful and accusing faces did rise before him, they made him feel despicable.

At midnight on February 19th, Tom was sinking into sleep in his rich bed, guarded by loyal servants and surrounded by royalty's splendors. He was happy because the next day was appointed for his solemn crowning as king of England. At that same hour Edward, the true king—hungry, thirsty, dirty, and roughed up by the riot—was wedged in a crowd watching the workmen who streamed in and out of Westminster Abbey, busy as ants. They were making the last preparations for the royal coronation.

CHAPTER 31

The Recognition Procession

When Tom awoke the next morning, the entire land was buzzing. It was music to him because it meant that the whole English world was out to welcome the great day.

Tom soon found himself the centerpiece of a wonderful floating parade on the Thames. By ancient custom the "recognition procession" through London had to start at the Tower, and he was on his way there. When he arrived, the old fortress was aglow with torchlight. An explosion of fireworks drowned the roar of the crowd and made the ground tremble. Jets of flame, billows of smoke, and loud cracks came in rapid succession. The Tower disappeared in a thick fog of smoke—except for the very top, which displayed banners and stood out like a mountain peak above clouds.

Splendidly decked out, Tom mounted a prancing warhorse whose rich decorations reached almost to the ground. His "uncle," the Lord Protector Somerset, took his place behind Tom on a similar horse. Clad in polished armor, the King's Guard lined up in one file on each side. Then followed a long procession of dazzling nobles and their servants. After these came the lord mayor and the local officials, in crimson velvet robes, gold chains across their chests. After these came the officers and members of all of London's guilds, in rich costumes and carrying showy banners. Also in the procession, as a special guard of honor through the city, was the Ancient and Honorable Artillery Company, the only military body in England outside Parliament's command. It presented a brilliant spectacle. People cheered as it marched through the packed crowd.

As Tom entered the city, the people welcomed him with prayers, cries, tender words, and expressions of earnest love. He smiled at those who stood far away and spoke tenderly to those who stood near. To those who said "God save his Grace," he replied, "God save you all" and added that he thanked them with all his heart. The people were thrilled with their king's loving answers and gestures.

In Fenchurch Street a young boy in a luxurious costume stood on a stage and recited a poem welcoming his majesty to the city, after which the crowd cheered. Tom gazed at the sea of eager faces, and his heart swelled with joy. He felt that the only thing worth living for was to be a king and a nation's idol. Then he caught sight, at a distance, of two of his ragged Offal Court friends— one of them, the Lord High Admiral in his pretend court; the other, the First Lord of the Bedchamber in the same game. If only he could let them know who he was! What unspeakable glory it would be if they realized that the ridiculed king of the slums had become a real king, with famous dukes and princes to serve him and the English world at his feet. But he had to deny this desire; such recognition might cost more than it was worth. So he looked away and left the two soiled lads to go on shouting, unaware of whom they were praising.

Every now and then, people cried, "Gift! Gift!" Tom responded by scattering a handful of bright new coins, which the people scrambled to grab.

At Gracechurch Street's upper end, the city had built a gorgeous arch. Beneath it was a stage that stretched from one side of the street to the other. On the stage were statues of the king's immediate ancestors. Elizabeth of York sat in the middle of an immense white rose whose petals formed an elaborate frame around her. By her side was Henry the Seventh, surrounded by a vast red rose. The royal pair held hands, their wedding rings prominently displayed. A stem from the flowers climbed to a second stage on which Henry the Eighth sat in the middle of a red-and-white rose, with the new king's mother, Jane Seymour, at his side. A stem from this pair climbed to a third stage, with a statue of Edward the Sixth on his throne. The whole scene was framed with wreaths of red and white roses. As Tom passed, the people saw how perfectly his face matched that of his statue, and rounds of applause broke out.

The great pageant moved under one triumphal arch after another. It passed a series of displays, each illustrating some virtue or talent of the little king. Throughout Cheapside, banners and streamers hung from every window. Rich carpets and gold cloths decorated the streets, showing the wealth of the local stores. "All these wonders and marvels are to welcome me—me!" Tom thought. The mock king's cheeks were flushed with excitement and pleasure.

Just as he was raising his hand to fling more coins, he caught sight of a pale, astounded face in the middle of the crowd, its intense eyes riveted on him. A sickening dismay went through him as he recognized his mother. His hand flew up, palm outward, before his eyes in that old involuntary gesture that was his habit. In an instant she had torn her way out of the crowd, past the guards, and was at his side. She embraced his leg, covered it with kisses, and cried, "Oh my child, my darling!" with a face full of joy and love. The same instant, an officer of the King's Guard snatched her away with a curse and sent her reeling back into the crowd. Tom was in the middle of saying "I do not know you, woman" when this occurred. It broke his heart to see her mistreated. As she turned for a last glimpse of him, she looked so wounded that shame turned his pride to ashes and withered his stolen royalty. His grand trappings seemed like rotten rags.

The procession moved on through greater

whirlwinds of welcome, but they were nothing to Tom. He neither saw nor heard. Filled with remorse, he thought, "If only I were free of my captivity." The shining pageant wound like an endless serpent down the quaint old city's crooked lanes. But the king rode with bowed head and vacant eyes, seeing only his mother's face and its wounded look.

"Gift! Gift!" The cry fell on deaf ears. "Long live Edward of England!" The loud chant was smothered by a voice, within Tom's conscience, that kept repeating the shameful words "I do not know you, woman." At every turn, new wonders sprang into view while artillery fired and crowds shouted their devotion, but Tom saw nothing except his mother's face and heard nothing except the accusing voice of his conscience.

After a while the crowds looked less happy, and their applause decreased. The Lord Protector was quick to notice. He rode to Tom's side, bent low in his saddle, and said, "My liege, the people observe your downcast head and clouded face. Lift up your face, and smile at the people." The duke scattered a handful of coins right and left, then returned to his place. The mock king mechanically did as he had been told. Without pleasure, he smiled, nodded graciously, saluted his subjects, and scattered coins. And the people praised him as loudly as before. Just before the procession ended, the duke was obliged to ride forward and remind Tom, "My sovereign, shake off your dark mood.

The world's eyes are on you." With sharp annoy-ance, he added, "To ruin with that crazy pauper! It was she who upset your highness."

Tom turned a dim eye on the duke and said in a dead voice, "She was my mother."

"My God," the Protector groaned as he reined his horse backward to his position. "He has gone mad again."

CHAPTER 32

Coronation Day

Let us go backward a few hours on that memorable Coronation Day. At three o'clock in the morning, when the warning guns boomed, London and Westminster started buzzing. By four o'clock Westminster Abbey's torch-lit galleries were filling with people willing to wait hours to see something they might see only once in their lives: the crowning of a king. Crowds of rich people who had bought seats in the galleries already were pouring in. When no space remained, all activity stopped for a while. The dim cathedral's galleries and balconies were full of people. The nave, the space near the altar, was empty and waiting for England's privileged ones.

The throne stood in the center of a large carpeted platform, four steps above the floor. Enclosed on the throne's seat was a rough flat rock, the Stone of Scone. Many generations of Scottish kings had sat on it to be crowned, and it now was used by English monarchs. The throne and its footstool were covered with gold cloth.

The hours dragged by. Finally, day returned, the torches were extinguished, and the cathedral glowed with sunlight softened by cloud cover. All of the building's noble features could be seen now.

At seven o'clock the first titled person entered the nave and was taken to her reserved place by an official wearing satin and velvet. A duplicate of him gathered up the lady's long train, followed her, and, when the lady was seated, arranged her train across her lap. He placed her footstool as she wanted it and put her small crown where she could reach it for the crowning of the nobles.

A glittering stream of titled ladies flowed in. Satin-clad officials flitted everywhere, seating them and making them comfortable. The scene was lively, with shifting color all around. After a time, quiet returned because the titled ladies all were in their places—an acre of human flowers, dazzling and diamond-frosted. All ages were represented. There were brown, wrinkled, white-haired heiresses who could recall Richard the Third's crowning. There were handsome middle-aged dames, lovely and gracious young matrons, and beautiful young girls with beaming eyes and fresh complexions. Because crowning was new to the young girls, their hair had been arranged to make putting on their crowns easy.

About nine o'clock the clouds broke away and a shaft of sunshine split the mellow atmosphere and slowly moved along the ranks of ladies. Every woman it touched flamed into a splendor of many-colored fire. Marching with other foreign ambassadors, an ambassador from some distant corner of the Orient crossed the bar of sunshine. He was covered with gems, so his slightest movement threw brightness all around him.

Time slowly passed: one hour, two hours, two and a half. Then the deep booming of artillery announced the arrival of the king and his grand procession. The waiting audience rejoiced.

Peers of the realm, in stately robes, ceremoniously were conducted to their seats; their crowns were placed within reach. The audience in the galleries was alive with interest; for most of them, this was the first glimpse of dukes, earls, and barons whose names had been famous for five hundred years. Robed heads of the Church and their attendants filed in and took their appointed places on the platform, followed by the Lord Protector, other great officials, and an armored group of guards. After a pause, a triumphant peal of music burst forth. Wearing a long gold robe, Tom Canty appeared at a door and stepped onto the platform.

The entire audience rose, and the Recognition ceremony began. An anthem swept the Abbey, welcoming Tom as he was led to the throne. The ancient ceremonies were solemnly conducted. As they neared completion, Tom grew paler and paler. His remorseful heart felt deepening distress. Finally, the Archbishop of Canterbury lifted England's crown from its cushion and held it over the head of the trembling mock king. Light flashed throughout the great nave as every noble lifted a crown and held it in the air over his or her head. A deep hush fell on the Abbey.

Suddenly a startling sight appeared, moving

up the great central aisle. It was a boy, bareheaded and clothed in coarse, ragged garments. He raised his hand with a seriousness that did not match his soiled and sorry appearance and delivered this warning: "I forbid you to set England's crown on the wrong head. I am the king!"

Several angry hands grabbed the boy. But in the same instant Tom stepped forward and cried in a ringing voice, "Let him go! He is the king!"

The shocked audience partly rose in their places and stared at one another like people who wonder whether they are dreaming or awake. The Lord Protector was as amazed as the rest but quickly recovered and exclaimed in a voice of authority, "Do not mind his majesty. His illness is on him again. Seize the beggar!"

He would have been obeyed, but the mock king stamped his foot and cried, "On your peril! Do not touch him. He is the king!"

The hands withdrew. No one moved or spoke. While people tried to make sense of the situation, the boy continued to move forward, with a confident expression. He stepped onto the platform, and Tom joyfully ran to meet him. Falling onto his knees before the king, Tom said, "My lord the king, let poor Tom Canty be the first to swear loyalty to you and say, 'Put on your crown and reclaim your throne!'"

The Lord Protector looked sternly at the newcomer, but his face immediately showed wonder. It was the same with the other great officers. They glanced at one another, thinking, "What a strange resemblance!" The Lord Protector reflected a moment, then said respectfully, "By your favor, sir, I would like to ask certain questions that..."

"I will answer them, my lord."

The duke asked the king many questions about the court, the late king, the prince, and the princesses. Without hesitation the boy answered them correctly. He described the palace's rooms of state, the late king's apartments, and those of the Prince of Wales. "It is remarkable," the Lord Protector said, "but it is no more than our lord the king can do. It proves nothing." He pondered for a time. Then his face lit up, and he confronted the ragged applicant with this question: "Where is the Great Seal? Only the true king knows the answer. The throne hangs on this question."

The great officials looked at one another with approval. Yes, none but the true king could solve the stubborn mystery of the vanished Great Seal. This ragged little impostor had learned his information well, but here he would fail because not even the Lord Protector could answer that question. Soon this troublesome and dangerous business would be over. They nodded with satisfaction and waited to see the impostor display guilty confusion.

How surprised they were when he promptly answered, in a confident voice, "There is nothing difficult about this question." Without hesitating, he turned and, with the easy manner of someone used to doing such things, gave this command: "My Lord St. John, go to my private apartment in the palace. No one knows the place better than you. Close to the floor, in the left corner farthest from the door, you will find a brass nail head in the wall. Press on the nail head, and a little jewel closet will fly open. No one in the world knows this little closet except me and the trusty artisan who made it for me. The first thing that you see will be the Great Seal. Bring it here."

Everyone wondered at this speech and the fact that the little beggar had picked out this noble without hesitation and called him by name as if he had known him all his life. Lord St. John started to go but then stopped, blushing. Tom turned to him and said sharply, "Why do you hesitate? Did you not hear the king's command? Go!" Lord St. John bowed deeply—not toward either king but at the neutral ground between the two—and left.

Like a turning kaleidoscope, glittering nobles slowly moved away from Tom and gathered again near the newcomer. During the suspenseful wait that followed, the few nobles remaining near Tom also glided, one by one, over to the majority. In his royal robes and jewels, Tom stood alone.

Lord St. John was seen returning. As he advanced up the aisle, the crowd's low murmur died out to a profound hush, so that his steps made a dull and distant sound. Every eye was fastened on him as he moved along. He reached the platform, paused a moment, bowed deeply before Tom, and said, "Sire, the Seal is not there."

Terrified, the band of courtiers shrank from the shabby little beggar as though he showed symptoms of the plague. In a moment he stood alone, the object of scornful and angry looks. The Lord Protector called out fiercely, "Throw the beggar into the street, and whip him through the town! The worthless liar needs no more consideration."

Officers of the guard sprang forward to obey, but Tom waved them off and declared, "Back!

Whoever touches him risks his life."

The Lord Protector was confused. "Did you search well?" he asked Lord St. John. "Small things easily get lost, but how can the Seal of England have vanished? How can something as noticeable as a large golden disk..."

"Wait!" Tom shouted, springing forward. "Was it round and thick? Did it have letters engraved on it? Yes? Oh, now I know what this Great Seal is. If you had described it to me, you could have had it three weeks ago. I know where it is, but I'm not the one who first put it there."

"Who, then, my liege?" the Lord Protector asked.

"He who stands there: England's rightful king. He himself will tell you where it is. Then you will believe that he knew. Think, my king. It was the last thing you did that day before you rushed out of the palace, clothed in my rags, to punish the soldier who had insulted me."

A silence fell. All eyes were fixed on the newcomer, who stood, with bent head and wrinkled brow, groping in his memory for one small, elusive fact that would seat him on a throne. Without it he would stay as he was, a pauper and an outcast. Moments became minutes. Still the boy struggled silently. At last he sighed, slowly shook his head, and said with a trembling lip and sad voice, "I can remember the scene, all of it, but not the Seal." He paused, then looked up and said with gentle dignity, "My lords and gentlemen, if you will rob your rightful king of his crown for lack of this evidence, I cannot stop you, but..."

"Oh folly! Oh madness, my king!" Tom cried. "Wait! Think! Do not give up. The cause is not lost. Listen to what I say. Follow every word. I am going to bring that morning back. We talked. I told you of my sisters, Nan and Bet—ah, you remember that—and about my old grandmother and the rough games of the Offal Court boys. Ah, you remember these things, too. You gave me food and drink and sent the servants away so that my table manners wouldn't embarrass me in front of them. Yes, you remember that also."

As Tom recited the details, and the other boy nodded his head in recognition, the audience stared in amazement. The tale sounded true, but how could this meeting between a prince and a beggar boy have occurred? "As a jest, my lord, we exchanged clothes. We stood before a mirror and said that it seemed as if no change had occurred. Yes, you remember that. Then you noticed that the soldier had hurt my hand—look, here is the wound; I cannot write with this hand yet because my fingers still are stiff. At this your highness sprang up, vowing revenge on the soldier, and ran toward the door. You passed a table, where that thing you call the Seal lay. You grabbed it and looked around eagerly, as if for a place to hide it. Your eye caught sight of..."

"Enough! Dear God be thanked!" the ragged king exclaimed in great excitement. "Go, my good

St. John. In an arm of the Milanese armor that hangs on the wall, you will find the Seal!"

"Right, my king! Right!" Tom cried. "Now England's scepter is yours. Go, Lord St. John. Give your feet wings!"

The whole audience was on its feet now, almost crazy with excitement and buzzing loudly with conversation. Time went by unnoticed. Then a hush fell over the house.

St. John appeared on the platform and held the Great Seal up in his hand! There was a great shout: "Long live the true king!" For five minutes the air shook with shouts and music and was white with a storm of waving handkerchiefs. In the center of the platform stood a ragged lad, the most famous person in England, flushed and proud, with the kingdom's great nobles kneeling around him.

Then all rose, and Tom said, "Now, my king, take these royal garments back, and give poor Tom, your servant, his rags again."

The Lord Protector said, "Let the rascal be stripped and flung into the Tower."

But the new king, the true king, said, "I will not have it so. If it weren't for him, I would not have regained my crown. No one will lay a hand on him. And as for you, my good uncle, my Lord Protector, your behavior is ungrateful toward this poor lad. I hear that he has made you a duke." The Protector blushed. "But he was not a king, so what is your fine title worth now? Tomorrow you will ask me, through him, for its confirmation.

Otherwise you will remain a simple earl." Under this rebuke his grace the Duke of Somerset retreated for the moment. The king turned to Tom and said kindly, "My poor boy, how was it that you could remember where I hid the Seal when I myself could not remember?"

"My king, that was easy because I used it a lot."

"You used it, but you could not explain where it was?"

"I did not know that it was the thing they wanted. They did not describe it, your majesty."

"Then, how did you use it?"

Tom blushed, lowered his eyes, and was silent.

"Speak up, good lad, and fear nothing," the king said. "How did you use the Great Seal of England?"

Tom stammered a moment, then got it out: "I used it... to crack nuts."

Poor child! The avalanche of laughter nearly swept him off his feet. If anyone had still believed that Tom Canty was England's rightful king, they believed this no more.

Meanwhile the sumptuous robe had been moved from Tom's shoulders to the king's. With the robe hiding the king's rags, the coronation resumed. The true king was anointed and crowned while cannons fired the news and all of London seemed to rock with applause.

CHAPTER 33

Edward as King

Miles Hendon was quite a sight before he got into the London Bridge riot, and he was more so when he got out of it—by which time, pickpockets had stripped him of his last farthing. No matter; he would find his boy. But how? Where would the boy naturally go? Being homeless and abandoned, he would go to his familiar places, Hendon reasoned. Where were his familiar places? His rags, combined with the low villain who claimed to be his father, indicated that his home was in one of London's poorest districts. Hendon would look for crowds in such districts. Sooner or later he would find his little friend in the center of a crowd entertaining itself by teasing the boy, who would be proclaiming himself king. Hendon would comfort and cheer him, and the two never would be separated again.

So Hendon started on his quest. Hour after hour he tramped through back alleys and squalid streets, seeking crowds. When daylight finally arrived, he had walked many miles and searched many crowds, but the only result was that he was tired and hungry. At noon he still was searching among the rabble who followed the royal procession. He thought that this regal display would powerfully attract his little lunatic. He followed the pageant through its twists and turns around London and all the way to Westminster and the Abbey. For a long time he drifted among the crowds, pondering what he should do.

When he came out of his thoughts, he discovered that Westminster was far behind him and the day was growing old. He was near the river and in the country, in a region of fine mansions. It wasn't cold, so he stretched himself on the ground near a hedge to rest and think. He heard the far-off boom of a cannon and thought, "The new king is crowned." Then, having not rested in more than thirty hours, he fell asleep.

He did not awake until mid-morning. He washed himself in the river, drank a pint or two of water, and trudged off toward Westminster, grumbling at himself for having wasted so much time. Hunger helped him form a new plan. He would try to speak with old Sir Humphrey Marlow and borrow a little money, and... That was enough of a plan for now.

Toward eleven o'clock he approached the palace. Although he was surrounded by people moving in the same direction as he was, he was conspicuous because of his shabby clothing. He looked closely at these people, hoping to spot someone who might be willing to carry his message to the old lieutenant. Trying to get into the palace himself was out of the question.

To rest where he still could see passersby, Hendon sat on a stone bench just outside the palace. He hardly had sat down when some ax-bearers and their commanding officer passed by. The officer saw him, halted his men, and ordered Hendon to come forward. He obeyed and promptly was arrested as a suspicious character prowling around the palace. Hendon started to explain, but the officer roughly silenced him and ordered his men to disarm and search him. They found nothing but a document. The officer tore it open, and Hendon recognized the "doodles" made by his little friend that black day at Hendon Hall. The officer's face darkened as he read the English paragraph out loud. Hendon paled as he listened. "Another new claimant to the crown!" the officer cried. "Men, seize the rascal and hold onto him while I take this paper to the king." He hurried away, leaving the prisoner in the grip of the ax-bearers.

"I will be hanged because of that paper," Hendon thought. "What will become of my poor lad? Only God knows."

The officer soon returned, in a great hurry. He ordered his men to release the prisoner and return his sword to him. Then he bowed respectfully and said, "Please follow me, sir."

Bewildered, Hendon followed. The two crossed a crowded courtyard and arrived at the palace's grand entrance. Here the officer, with another bow, delivered Hendon into the hands of another official, who received him with deep respect and led him through a great hall. The corridor was lined with rows of splendid attendants, who bowed as the two passed. But the attendants fell into fits of silent laughter the moment the raggedy Hendon had passed. The two men went up a broad staircase, past more people, and into a vast room. The official parted the way for him through England's assembled nobility, then bowed and reminded him to take off his hat. He left him standing in the middle of the room, the target of annoyed looks.

The king sat under a royal canopy five steps away, speaking with a sort of human bird of paradise, maybe a duke. Hendon thought that it was hard enough to be sentenced to death in the prime of life without also having this public humiliation. He wished that the king would hurry.

The king raised his head slightly, and Hendon got a good view of his face. The sight nearly took his breath away. He stared at the king and thought, "Am I dreaming? Can it be? Is he truly England's sovereign and not the poor, friendless Tom of Bedlam I took him for?"

An idea flashed in his mind. He strode to the wall, picked up a chair, brought it back, planted it on the floor, and sat down. A buzz of indignation broke out, a rough hand was laid on him, and a voice exclaimed, "Up, you rude clown! Would you sit in the presence of the king?"

The disturbance attracted the attention of his majesty, who stretched out his hand and cried, "Do

not touch him! It is his right." The crowd fell back, amazed. The king went on: "Ladies, lords, and gentlemen, this is my trusty and well-loved servant Miles Hendon, who used his good sword and saved me from bodily harm and possible death. For this he is a knight, by the king's command. Also, for the higher service of saving his sovereign from lashes and shame and taking these upon himself, he is declared Earl of Kent. He will have gold and lands suited to this honor. Moreover, the privilege of sitting in my presence is his by royal grant. I have declared that the sons of his line will have the right to sit in the presence of England's majesty forever more. Do not disturb him."

Two people who had arrived five minutes before stood listening to these words and looking at the king and Hendon in bewilderment. These were Sir Hugh and Lady Edith.

But the new earl did not see them. He still was

staring at the monarch in a dazed way. "Oh! This is my pauper," he said to himself. "This is my lunatic. This is he to whom I would show what grandeur is, with my house of seventy rooms and twenty-seven servants. This is he who never had known anything but rags for clothing, kicks for comfort, and garbage for dinner. This is he whom I adopted and would make respectable. God give me a bag in which to hide my head!"

As soon as his wits returned to him, so did his manners. He dropped to his knees, swearing allegiance and thanking the king for his lands and titles. Then he rose and stood respectfully aside, with many envious eyes on him.

Now the king noticed Sir Hugh and said angrily, "Strip this robber of his stolen estates, and put him under lock and key until I have need of him." Sir Hugh was led away.

There was a stir at the room's other end. The crowd fell apart and Tom Canty, modestly but finely clothed, marched out preceded by a servant. He knelt before the king, who said, "I have learned the story of these past few weeks, and I am well pleased with you. You have governed with royal gentleness and mercy. You have found your mother and sisters again? Good. They will be cared for, and your father will hang if you desire it and the law agrees. All who hear my voice, know that from this day forward those who live in Christ's Hospital and share the king's wealth will have their minds and hearts fed, as well as their stomachs. This boy will live there and head its honorable officials. Because he has been a king, he will command special treatment. He will have his own costume, which no one may copy. Wherever he goes, his dress will remind people that he once was royal, and no one will deny him reverence. He has the throne's protection and the crown's support. He will be known by the honorable title of the King's Ward."

Proud and happy, Tom rose and kissed the king's hand. As soon as he was conducted from the room, he ran to tell his mother, Nan, and Bet the great news.

CHAPTER 34

Justice and Punishment

All remaining mysteries were cleared up. The day that Miles had come to Hendon Hall, Hugh had threatened to have Lady Edith killed if she admitted knowing Miles. She had responded that he *should* take her life, then; she would not turn Miles away. Then Hugh had said that he would spare her life but have Miles killed unless she denied knowing him. To protect Miles, she then had agreed to the lie.

Hugh was not prosecuted for his threats or for stealing Miles's land and title because Lady Edith and Miles would not testify against him. He deserted Lady Edith and went to the continent, where he soon died. Soon after, Miles married Lady Edith. The village of Hendon rejoiced when the couple paid their first visit to the Hall.

Tom Canty's father never was heard of again.

The king found the farmer who had been branded and sold as a slave. He took him from his evil life with the Ruffler's gang and gave him a comfortable livelihood. He also got the old lawyer out of prison and returned his fine. He provided good homes for the daughters of the two Baptist women whom he had seen burned at the stake and severely punished the official who had laid the undeserved stripes on Miles's back. He saved the woman who had stolen cloth from a weaver and the boy who had taken the falcon. But he was too late to save the man who had been convicted of killing a deer in the royal forest. He showed favor to the judge who had pitied him when he was convicted of stealing a piglet; he was pleased to see the judge grow popular with the people and become a great and honored man.

As long as the king lived, he was fond of telling the story of his adventures, from the hour that the guard knocked him away from the palace gate until the final midnight when he blended in with a group of hurrying workmen and so slipped into the Abbey, where he hid himself in a tomb and then slept so long the next day that he almost missed the coronation. He said that frequently telling the story reminded him of its lessons, which would benefit his people. By keeping his tale's sorrowful events fresh in his memory, he kept compassion strong in his heart.

Miles Hendon and Tom Canty were favorites of the king during his brief reign, and they deeply mourned him when he died. The Earl of Kent had too much good sense to abuse his peculiar privilege of sitting in the king's presence, but he exercised it twice more: once at Queen Mary's coronation and once at Queen Elizabeth's. A descendant of his exercised the privilege at James the

First's coronation. By the time this descendant's son chose to exercise the privilege—nearly twenty-five years later—most people had forgotten the "privilege of the Kents." So, when the Kent of that day appeared before Charles the First and his court and sat down in the king's presence, there was quite a stir. But soon the matter was explained and the right confirmed. The line's last earl fell in the wars of the Commonwealth, fighting for the king, and the odd privilege ended with him.

Tom lived to be very old, a handsome, white-haired fellow with a serious and kind face. As long as he lived, he was honored. His striking costume reminded people that he once had been royal. Wherever he appeared the crowd fell apart, making way for him and whispering, "Take off your hat. It is the King's Ward!" They saluted and were honored to get his kindly smile in return.

King Edward the Sixth lived only a few years, but he lived them well. Whenever some dignitary would argue against his leniency, saying that some law was not too harsh and didn't inflict unreasonable suffering, the young king would turn his compassionate eyes on him and say, "What do you know of suffering and oppression? I and my people know, but not you." Edward the Sixth's reign was an unusually merciful one for those harsh times. For that, we owe him gratitude.

AFTERWORD

About the Author

One of the themes of the novel *The Prince and the Pauper* is the journey from riches to rags, and back again. Mark Twain knew this journey well, having been both poor and wealthy at various stages in his life. Although he is possibly the most successful American writer, he lost his fortune in the middle of his career and went deeply into debt. He would eventually use his talent and reputation to come out on top again.

Mark Twain, whose real name was Samuel Clemens, was born November 30, 1835 in a two-room shack in Missouri, the sixth child of John and Jane Clemens. The Clemens family soon moved to Hannibal, a small town on the edge of the Mississippi. Here, Sam had a childhood full of pranks, fights and fun on the river. He would later use these memories as the basis for his novel *Tom Sawyer*.

His mother was a lively and spontaneous woman, interested in everything. But his father was the opposite — cold and distant — and he didn't show Sam affection. He had trained as a lawyer, but he could never earn much money. He failed at nearly everything he tried, and he wasted most of his energies on unlikely schemes, including a perpetual motion machine and silkworm farming. Although the Clemenses had slaves when Sam was very young, they gradually lost all of them because of their poverty. His mother began cooking for other families to bring in money. When Sam was 11, his father died of pneumonia, and Jane Clemens continued to support herself and her children still at home, including Sam.

Two years after his father's death, Sam was apprenticed to the printer of the *Missouri Courier*, a weekly newspaper. He learned how to typeset, and he consequently read everything that went into the paper. He began writing his own material, and at age 16, he published a story in the *Carpetbag*, a national humor magazine. He also worked for the *Hannibal Journal and Western Union*, a paper run by his brother Orion. Unfortunately, his brother was a poor businessman, and Sam realized that the paper would soon fail. He decided to take his skill on the road as a journeyman. For the next few years, he traveled to St. Louis, New York and Philadelphia, eventually returning to the Midwest to work at several papers.

By this time, Sam had developed the strong personality that would shape the course of his life. He was an extremely sensitive person, and as a result, he suffered and rejoiced more intensely than most. Injustice, cruelty, and oppression deeply disturbed him. He also tended to be careless, since he didn't like details, and he frequently acted impulsively. One of the best examples of his sudden decisions was when he left for the Amazon River in 1857, determined to seek his fortune. On the way to New Orleans, however, he met a steamboat pilot, and Sam convinced him to take him on as an apprentice. He stayed on the river to learn a new trade, his dreams of the Amazon abandoned.

For the next two years, he worked to earn his pilot's license. His younger brother, Henry, followed him by becoming a clerk on the steamboat *Pennsylvania*. But Henry was burned when the *Pennsylvania* caught fire, and he eventually died from his wounds. Sam was devastated and blamed himself for getting his brother interested in the steamboat life.

Sam kept working as a pilot until the Civil War broke out in 1861. He briefly formed a home guard in Missouri, but it soon disbanded, and he couldn't maintain any enthusiasm for the war. So he went west with Orion to Nevada, where his brother had been made territorial secretary for his loyalty to Abraham Lincoln. Sam worked for a month as a clerk, but the possibility of striking it rich with a gold or silver mine was irresistible. His efforts failed, however, and he ended up working in a quartz mill to survive.

While working at the mines, he had been sending humorous letters to the leading local newspaper. When its editors offered him a job as a reporter for $25 a week, he jumped at the chance. It was during this time that he settled on a pen name. The term "by the mark twain" was from the language of the Mississippi River. It referred to water that was two fathoms deep, safe enough for a steamboat to pass. In his new job, "Mark Twain" learned the reporting trade quickly, for there was lots of news in Virginia City — fights and other violence, and mining strikes. But he soon realized that readers wanted fantastic stories more than plain news, even if the stories were embellished or invented. Fortunately, this was the kind of writing he could do well and would excel at all his life.

He ended his career in Nevada by challenging an editor to a duel. Because dueling was illegal in that state, he left to avoid prosecution, going to San Francisco in 1864. He spent a short time as an urban reporter, but he felt miserable in that job. He eventually left and spent the next two years scratching out a living as a freelance writer. During this part of his life, he was deeply in debt and on the point of suicide. But he kept going on the hope that he could succeed as a writer of humorous material. He contributed to the magazine the *Californian*, which reprinted his articles in the Eastern papers. He also met the famous writer Bret Harte, who encouraged him to continue writing. Eventually, his persistence and belief in his talents paid off. In November 1865, his story "Jim Smiley and his Jumping Frog" was printed by the *New York Saturday Press*, and Mark Twain was recognized as one of the best American humorists.

This recognition opened up many opportunities. Twain was able to publish his first book of stories, although it earned him no money, and to write travel pieces. Various newspapers sent him to the Hawaiian Islands, Europe, and the Middle East. He sent back letters for publication, describing his impressions of the land and culture. His observations were often sarcastic and irreverent, and told in a humorous way. Because of the popularity of his travel pieces, he was approached by the American Publishing Company in Hartford, Connecticut. Its publisher gave him a contract for a travel book, with royalty payments. The book would be sold on subscription, which meant that orders would be taken door-to-door before publication. Twain used his travel articles as the basis of the book, and wrote the rest in a San Francisco hotel room. He titled it *The Innocents Abroad.*

That same year, 1869, he met and fell in love with Olivia Langdon, the sister of a friend. She came from a wealthy coal family, and her parents were skeptical of Twain as a potential husband. But he would not give up, and eventually they accepted him as a son-in-law. She helped him proofread the galleys of *Innocents* and became his personal editor, a role she would fill until she died. The book sold extremely well. On the day before their wedding, in 1870, Twain received a royalty check for more than $4,000.

Olivia's father gave them a house in Buffalo,

but they soon moved to Hartford. Their marriage had a difficult beginning: her father passed away, and then her close friend died while staying at the Clemens' house. Their first child was born prematurely and died within two years. Then they had a daughter, Susy, in 1872, and Twain took his wife and new daughter to England, where he lectured and did research. When they returned to Hartford, they moved into a new mansion. It would be their home for 17 years. The house became a meeting place for many literary types, including Twain's neighbor, Harriet Beecher Stowe, who had written *Uncle Tom's Cabin*.

In 1873, Twain published *The Gilded Age*. One of its characters, Colonel Sellers, was a dreamer, always latching on to the next get-rich-quick scheme. By creating Sellers, Twain had tapped into a popular American mentality, one he had seen in his father, his cousin, and certainly himself. For years, Twain invested in a variety of disastrous ventures, including the invention of a typesetting machine, which cost him over $200,000. The only venture of Twain's that succeeded was the publication of the Ulysses S. Grant memoirs, which rescued Grant's widow from poverty.

During the next several years, Twain published *Tom Sawyer*, *The Prince and the Pauper*, *Life on the Mississippi* (recollections of his life as a steamboat pilot), and his most famous book, *Huckleberry Finn*. He traveled with his friend

Joseph Twichell in Germany and the Alps, and their journey was the basis for Twain's novel, *A Tramp Abroad*. His second child, Clara, was born in 1874, and another daughter, Jean, arrived in 1880.

In 1891, the Clemens family finally faced the fact that they could not afford their rich lifestyle. Twain's various business ventures had drained the accounts. They decided to close their mansion and move to Berlin, where they could live more cheaply. In fact, they lived all over Europe — in France, Germany, Italy, and Switzerland. By 1894, they were bankrupt and $100,000 in debt.

Twain had grown to hate lecturing and had vowed never to do it again. But in order to repay his debts, he began a world reading tour in 1895, at the age of sixty. His creditors had offered to accept only half of what he owed, but he and his wife wanted to repay the full amount. They set out on the journey with their daughter Clara, leaving the others at home.

The Clemenses visited Australia, New Zealand, India and South Africa, then England. The readings were a great success, and brought in a lot of money. But at the end of the tour they received word in England that their daughter Susy was ill with meningitis. Olivia and Clara sailed at once for home, but while they were traveling, Twain received word that Susy had died. He couldn't get home in time for the funeral. His wife and daughter returned after Susy had been buried, and they stayed through the winter in London. Twain worked on *Following the Equator*, an account of his world lecture tour. The profits from this book, combined with his lecture fees, paid off his debts entirely.

The Clemenses stayed in Europe, living in Vienna and England. When they finally returned to the U.S. in 1900, Twain received a celebrated welcome. His debts had been paid, and his fame was greater than ever. However, this happy time would not last long. Olivia soon became seriously ill, and in the fall of 1903, they traveled to Florence, Italy to be in a warmer climate. She died several months later. Twain had lost his true love and his most dedicated editor.

Although Twain had never been formally educated, he had honorary degrees from Yale and the University of Missouri. But perhaps the high point of his career was accepting a prestigious doctor's robe from Oxford in 1907. When he visited England to receive the degree, he could hardly walk down the street without being greeted and surrounded by admirers. It took two secretaries to handle his visitors and letters.

Twain's popularity stemmed partly from his success as a lecturer. His wit and spontaneity made him an exciting and entertaining speaker. But he was mainly loved for his articles, stories, and sketches. His work made people laugh, but it was also full of wisdom, compassion, and lasting truth. Because Twain was an expert on human nature, his characters were extremely believable, and his readers could relate to them. Twain was especially concerned with moral issues, and often used his writing to draw attention to hypocrisy and oppression. He coined many famous moral sayings, such as "When in doubt, tell the truth."

Twain had been born during the appearance of Haley's Comet, which is visible from the Earth only once every 75 years. He and the comet had come into the world together, and Twain had said that they "must go out together." After spending his old age at a house in Connecticut, where he read, wrote, and played billiards, his time had finally come. He died of heart problems in April of 1910, the year Haley's Comet returned to the skies.

About the Book

The Prince and the Pauper was published in 1881, and the book sold only 17,000 copies. Compared to Mark Twain's other novels, this one was not a success. The public may have thought it too serious, with too much social commentary. Certainly, it is not as humorous as some of his other stories. However, some critics did admire it, including the writer Harriet Beecher Stowe. She called the novel "The best book for young folks ever written." Twain's family loved the book, and thought it was his best work. Twain himself enjoyed writing it so much that he didn't want it to end.

The Clemens family would be happy to know that Twain's "best work" enjoys more popularity today. It has been adapted for cinema, television, theater, and children's literature. Though it has never been praised as much as Twain's *Tom Sawyer* or *Huckleberry Finn*, *The Prince and the Pauper* still entertains and educates readers, and for many reasons.

One of the novel's simplest attractions is that it indulges a fantasy many people have about suddenly becoming rich. Tom Canty, who has dreamed about being a prince all of his young life, suddenly finds himself living as a real prince in a palace. He is surrounded by wealth and power, and servants attend to his every wish. It seems that Tom's dreams have come true.

Twain doesn't let Tom, or the reader, off the hook so easily, however. He shows us that wealth and power are more complicated than we might think. Tom soon realizes that the palace is a sort of prison, for he cannot do anything for himself, and no one will believe that he isn't the prince. It looks like he will be trapped in the palace forever. Longingly, he remembers the freedom he enjoyed in the outside world, where he could run and play with his friends, safe from responsibility.

Prince Edward, on the other hand, experiences what many people fear: going from rich to poor. Accustomed to being pampered, Edward must learn how to survive on his wits and little else. As a prince in the beginning of the story, he envies the freedom of ordinary citizens like Tom: "If only I could dress in clothes like yours, and bare my feet, and play in the mud once, just once, with no one to scold or forbid me, I believe I could give up the crown!" While living as a pauper, however, Edward soon finds that the reality is very different. He has to endure hunger, injustice, and humiliation. Although he thinks that he has fallen as low as he can go, he meets others who have it even worse. He is shocked and surprised to learn that some people's lives are full of violence and persecution. This knowledge later makes him a more just and compassionate king.

Indeed, Twain used the story as an opportunity to describe many of the cruelties and injustices common in sixteenth century England. He lists a number of punishments that were given out regularly: branding, boiling in oil, cutting off ears, burning at the stake. This was Twain's first historical novel, and it was carefully researched. He wanted to make people aware of the horrific tortures that were practiced during that time period.

Twain also used the story to express his opinion about royalty. For example, when describing how the servants dress Tom, he creates a funny image of a pair of hose being passed down a long line of people. Was that the way things were actually done? Probably not, but it shows how ridiculous Twain thought royal customs were. In fact, some people considered the novel to be a protest against the monarchy.

None of these educational or political points would be very interesting without good characters, however. Tom and Edward capture the reader's imagination because they are fully developed. Switching their identities is more than just an entertaining gimmick — it is a way to show what the boys are really made of. As Edward and Tom each react to their challenging circumstances, the reader can more easily see their redeeming (or not so redeeming) qualities. While no one in the story can tell a difference between the two boys, the reader can tell a lot of difference!

Edward starts out as a haughty, spoiled prince with few skills he can use to survive on his own.

But as the story progresses, we see how brave and resourceful he can be. For example, when he gets scared by the calf in the barn, he faces his fear instead of shrinking from it. Then he uses the calf as a way to keep warm, which many people might not have thought to do. As a result of showing his good qualities, Edward is transformed from a spoiled brat into a brave underdog, the type of character that readers love to cheer for.

Tom begins the story as a poor, romantic, but unsophisticated beggar. He doesn't seem to do much of anything; instead, things happen to him. But as he becomes more comfortable in the palace, he asserts himself by reviewing and correcting criminal punishments. The reader discovers that he is not only compassionate, but also wise. Having power brings out the best in Tom instead of the worst.

The Prince and the Pauper also appeals to us as a story about growing up. Both boys go through hardships — some mental, some physical — that teach them various lessons about themselves and other people. They experience abandonment, isolation, loss of family, and of course, adventure. These experiences help them to develop the qualities they lack: Edward learns compassion, patience, and humility, while Tom learns loyalty, responsibility, and composure. Both boys see things and people that broaden their sense of the world, which is an important part of leaving childhood behind.

If we choose to see the novel as a growing-up story, then *The Prince and Pauper* shows us that the final act of becoming an adult is to claim one's true identity. Is it any coincidence that young people often leave home "find themselves"? At the end of the story, both Edward and Tom go back to being their true selves, though they have each changed for the better.

The idea of true identity is certainly an interesting theme of the book. Twain gives us lots of chances to think about it. He shows us how identity is easily confused by clothing, speech and behavior. What, then, is a true sign of identity? What makes us who we are?

One way to answer this question is to look at Tom and Edward's journeys. What is it that pushes them to reclaim their identities? In Edward's case, it is loyalty to his crown. He knows that it is his duty to be king. In Tom's case, it is loyalty to his mother. Seeing her in the crowd reminds him of the person he really is. In the end, he decides that he wants to be that person again.

Perhaps Twain is saying that the people and things we care about make us who we are, not the amount of money we have or the clothes we wear. When Tom and Edward are true to what and whom they love, everything is put right again. From this, we could deduce that being your true self is not only fulfilling, it is necessary for society to function properly. Restoring the prince and pauper's identities also restores order to the realm. And that gives us yet another reason to enjoy this tale: a happy ending.